ΛCHE

HELLISH #6

CHARITY PARKERSON

Ache
Hellish, #6
Charity Parkerson

--Warning: This book is intended for readers over the age of 18.

Editor: Hercules & Consultants

ISBN-13: 978-1-946099-39-6

ISBN-10: 1-946099-39-2

❀ Created with Vellum

INTRODUCTION

DAMAGED DOESN'T BEGIN TO COVER
TAMIL'S CURRENT STATE. RISKEL WANTS TO
FIX THAT.

Turned out at a young age, Tamil was taken in by evil. All he's known is abuse until Jonathan comes to his rescue. His mind and body are broken, but Jonathan's home is different from any place he's ever been. People are kind for no reason. As much as that messes with his head, it's nothing compared to the way Riskel confuses him. Nothing feels real anymore.

Even though Tamil almost killed Riskel, Riskel knows a wounded beast when he sees one—in pain and lashing out. Riskel can't stop himself from trying to help. Each day he gains Tamil's trust a little more —like taming a wild animal. Only time will tell if Tamil is worth the effort or if he'll slice Riskel's throat in his sleep. It's a chance Riskel's willing to take.

Unfortunately, Riskel isn't the only being obsessed with Tamil. Evil doesn't want to let go. Riskel will have to risk more than his neck if he hopes to break the devil's hold.

PROLOGUE

THIS BOOK HAS ALL THE TRIGGERS. ALL OF THEM. Tamil's story is hard, but like a lot of us, it's his story to tell.

He was little more than a child. Riskel wasn't sure where to go with that knowledge. The anger over being brutally beaten and left for dead ran deep. Still, Riskel had a hard time clinging to his rage as he watched Tamil sleep. As a shape shifter, Tamil could take any form. He was dangerous. Whatever form he assumed, he could mimic their abilities. As their king, Jonathan should've either let Tamil die when Evan tore out his throat or finished the job. Child or not, Tamil could potentially destroy them all.

While unconscious, Tamil had reverted to his true form. He was probably no more than nineteen. Blond and angelic. His beauty had Riskel moving closer. He probed at the boy's mind, trying to see why such a sweet and innocent-looking being had become such a monster as to attack Riskel, kidnap Evan, and chain Bleidd in silver. Bleidd—most likely —deserved his punishment. But Riskel knew nothing of Tamil, and Evan was too sweet to fall victim to such violence. The inside of Tamil's mind was blank. Inky darkness devoid of emotion or hope. Riskel pulled away, incapable of tolerating more than a second of the boy's suffering. It took him a moment to realize sky-blue eyes—like a summer's day, were focused upon him. They were dead.

"Have you decided whether you'll kill me?" Tamil's voice sounded hoarse, as if it hurt to speak.

As the question sank in, Riskel realized he held his knife. He moved closer. It went against his nature to watch an animal suffer. Tamil should be put down. It was the merciful choice. Tamil didn't budge. He made no move to defend himself nor did he beg for his life. He simply waited—accepting. Relieved.

Tamil reached for him, slowly, as if expecting Riskel to lash out. His warm fingers encircled Riskel's wrist. He urged Riskel even closer, pressing the blade to his own throat. At the artery. As a vampire, Riskel could smell the man's blood. Hear his heart rate. There was no scent of fear. His heart beat steady.

"It's okay," Tamil said, wooing him with his voice. "No one will miss me. It's for the best. He'll come for me, and I won't go back." Still, Riskel couldn't do it. It didn't matter the boy had nearly killed him. He'd certainly left Riskel for dead. No strength would enter his arm, making the cut needed to end Tamil's life. "Here," Tamil said, still sounding calm. "I'll get you started." He pressed the knife harder against his throat. A thin line of blood appeared beneath the blade. Tamil didn't flinch or back down. "It's time."

An explosion of movement blew through the room. Riskel found himself shoved aside. Jonathan pounced, covering Tamil's body with his. His wings glowed bright, hiding Tamil's body, protecting him. Riskel couldn't look away from Tamil's face, even as someone dragged him away. The boy's eyes were full of tears and disappointment. He'd wanted to die, and Jonathan had stolen his chance at peace.

"Get him out of here." Jonathan's yelled demand barely penetrated the trance Tamil weaved over him. The hands pulling at his body couldn't break the spell.

Riskel's throat swelled. He knew, as long as he lived, he'd never forget Tamil's devastation. He'd never unsee the pain. He stared at the closed bedroom door. Lire and Dougal tried talking to him, but he didn't hear a thing. Nothing penetrated the roar inside his ears until Jonathan reappeared. Sound came rushing back, nearly blasting out his eardrums. He closed the door behind him. His gaze locked on Riskel with fury. Riskel couldn't move. All he could do was stand there as Jonathan ate up the floor between them.

"What the hell is wrong with you? You're a guest in my home."

He was. Riskel couldn't even defend himself. Since Dougal found him on the edge of the property beaten half to death, he'd been staying with the king. "You're right. I didn't realize."

Jonathan's eyes glowed and swirled—like a pot of leprechaun gold. He grew taller by the moment as he hovered over Riskel, appearing ready to pounce. His fury obviously wasn't assuaged. "Which part didn't you realize? That you're a guest here?"

"That he is broken." Even Riskel heard the regret in his tone. When he'd learned his attacker was under the same roof, Riskel hadn't thought. He'd gone on the attack.

Riskel's answer seemed to give Jonathan pause. He deflated a hair. His wings shrank. One of his eyes turned green, fascinating Riskel. He gave Risk a short nod. "Exactly." His voice softened. "We have the chance to right a great wrong here."

"Then you should do the merciful thing." Even Riskel heard the hard note in his voice. Sometimes the right thing wasn't the easy thing.

Jonathan shook his head. "He is a person, Risk. He can be helped. I refuse to lose my humanity in the face of such a travesty. Just as I do with everyone, I see inside his heart. Where it counts, he is still whole. I won't give up and I will *not* let anyone harm him again. You have two choices," Jonathan said, holding up two fingers. "You can leave and never darken my door again or you can stay and swear to do no harm."

"I won't hurt him." Riskel meant it. "After looking in his eyes, I'd already realized I couldn't do it."

"That's good," Jonathan said, taking a step back. "I have too much to do as it is without having to guard you too."

From the short time Riskel had been staying with the king, he'd seen that was true. He didn't know how the man had time to breathe. Lately, Jonathan had mentioned having visions of evil headed their way. Riskel had agreed to stay after he'd healed to do what he could. If Jonathan sensed danger, Riskel believed. The man was Goddess Celeste's grandson and a Nephilim. His powers were beyond what anyone could conceive. Riskel imagined he could end the world with the snap of his fingers. He didn't want to find out firsthand by pissing him off any further. "You have my word. I'll help you with the boy." God help him. He didn't know how, but he would.

Jonathan eyed him for a moment as if reading Riskel's every thought. "I believe you. It's almost time to eat. Join us. We'll have a family meeting afterward."

Riskel nodded while Jonathan headed back inside Tamil's room. He looked around at the men who waited with him. They were large men. Four Scottish warriors and a demon. Dougal and Faolan were mated to the Demon, Lire. It was an odd trio as far as Riskel was concerned, but it seemed to work for them. The other two warriors, Cin and Niall, were mated to the king. Riskel had no idea how he'd come to be here, but it seemed he was now one of the family. He recognized it as an honor, even as it felt like a curse.

WHEN THE BEDROOM DOOR REOPENED, Tamil moved to a sitting position. He'd already been caught being too comfortable once. Jonathan ducked inside the room. The man looked as if he'd grown since he'd left no more than two minutes earlier. Tamil's skin had already healed from the cut. It was a minor thing, yet Jonathan acted as if Tamil had lost an arm. Tamil had done that before too. As a shapeshifter, things always grew back. He knew. It had been one of Draven's favorite ways to torture him. A tiny slice across his neck was nothing. It definitely wasn't worth an ounce of rage.

"It's time to eat. Dougal cooked."

Tamil eyed Jonathan, unsure how to react. "Okay."

Jonathan waved for him to follow. "Come on. We're eating in the kitchen."

After shifting to his feet, Tamil followed Jonathan at a slow pace. He was a prisoner. It didn't make sense for Jonathan to invite him to eat with his clan. Maybe it was a new form of torment, forcing him to sit with people who hated him. Having eyes on him was a horrible punishment. Everyone always looked at him like he was an animal. Hell, maybe he was. In the kitchen, Tamil chose a chair off to the side, at the end of the table, and away from everyone else. Jonathan set a plate in front of him. He barely spared it a glance. Tamil had learned years ago that no one fed him without expecting something in return. He'd also learned to save as much as possible for later because he never knew when he'd eat again. Someone filled the chair across from him. Tamil risked a quick glance before returning his gaze to his lap. It was Riskel. Even though he wasn't looking Tamil's way, Tamil's anxiety skyrocketed. He grabbed his dinner roll when no one was looking and shoved it in his pocket. Tamil chanced a look around, ensuring he hadn't been seen. No one looked his way.

His stomach growled. The smell of food made him weak. He couldn't decipher these people's intentions. It was possible they would take his food away the moment they caught him eating. On the sly, he eyed the plate again, trying to decide what else he could hide. There was another roll on his plate. Tamil blinked. He was certain there'd only been one piece of bread earlier. After another quick check to ensure he wasn't seen, Tamil shoved the second roll in his pocket. Still, he wouldn't eat with so many people around. The danger was too great. He'd lost a hand more than once for believing he would be freely fed.

"You should eat," Jonathan said, sounding kind. "These guys aren't likely to leave you seconds."

Tamil kept his head bowed. He didn't trust this. Starvation had his gaze sliding back toward his plate. There was another roll on his plate. He wasn't imagining things. No one had come near him. It was like magic. He sneaked a peek at Riskel. His gaze was locked on his own plate, but he wasn't eating either. The sight firmed his belief he shouldn't touch the food. Everyone else stood. Tamil withdrew further, hardening his heart. They'd take the food now.

"When you two are finished and ready, come join us in the front room. Okay?"

Tamil didn't look away from his lap, but he nodded. They left him alone with Riskel. No one took his plate. Riskel stood and moved to the sink. With Riskel's back turned and Tamil free of anyone watching, he shoved some food in his mouth. He nearly choked as he tried swallowing without chewing. Still, Riskel didn't look his way. He shoved some more in his mouth. Not only did he not know what he was eating, he didn't care. It would sustain him. As Riskel came back to the table, Tamil curled inside himself, trying to hide the fact that he was chewing.

"Take these," Riskel said, pushing a few plastic bags his way. One was empty. The other had cookies inside. "Put your rolls in the empty one. They'll stay good longer that way."

Tamil didn't know how to react. His plate was empty, making him realize he'd eaten everything. Disappointment stirred in his gut. He fought the burning sensation behind his eyes. It could be weeks before he ate again, and he was scared to touch the cookies. Riskel swapped his full plate for Tamil's empty one.

"You can have mine too. I live mostly off blood. Food lost its appeal a hundred years ago."

There it was. The catch. Tamil forced his arm from where it clutched his stomach and flattened it on the table, wrist up. "You can have mine." Even to Tamil's ears, his voice shook. He ground his back teeth, hoping to make the shaking stop. Riskel made no move to drink from him. Tamil swallowed. "I probably don't taste very good." He couldn't imagine anyone wanting to drink from him.

"You're still recovering. I went hunting last night, so I'm okay. You should save your strength."

Tamil withdrew his arm and went back to holding himself. "My blood is dirty." He didn't know why he couldn't simply be relieved Riskel hadn't bitten him.

"I can smell your blood. There's nothing wrong with it. You do need to eat, though. You're malnourished."

His insides shook. Tamil wanted to accept Riskel's offer, but it didn't make sense. He'd hurt the man. Left him for dead. There was no reason for Riskel to show him kindness.

"Okay. Let's do this," Riskel said, shifting to his feet. He moved to the fridge and inspected the contents.

Tamil shoved food in his mouth, choking it down. Riskel went from the fridge to the cabinets. Tamil ate as fast as he could, risking making himself sick. As Riskel returned to the table, Tamil went back to staring at his lap. "Well, I'd planned to cover your plate, so you could take it with you, but it looks like you've almost finished."

"I'm sorry," Tamil said automatically. He couldn't control the fear in his voice and he fucking hated that.

"Don't apologize. You can finish. I'll wait with you. In fact, I won't watch." He turned sideways in his chair and stared at the wall.

Tamil tried taking another bite. His stomach revolted from eating too fast. He dropped his hands to his lap.

"Did food really lose its appeal?" Tamil hated to ask, but he needed to know if Riskel lied.

Riskel turned his head before Tamil had time to look away. Their gazes met. The man's eyes were like amber whiskey. He knew their color as well as his own since he'd spent weeks mimicking him. Still, their beauty caught him off guard.

"I used to be a slave," Riskel said instead of answering. "Back when I was human," he tacked on unnecessarily. "I used to dream about the rich foods my master would eat while I ate hard bread or not at all. After I killed my master, I overindulged quite often. Now I'm tired of everything, especially since I don't need it to survive. Why are your wrists scarred? Shifters shouldn't scar."

Tamil blinked at the subject change. He went back to staring at his lap. "Shifters scar under the right circumstances. How did you kill your master?"

Riskel stood. "If you don't plan to finish eating, we'd better join the meeting so Jonathan can tell everyone what's going on. Sit with me at the next meal, and maybe I'll tell you the story about how I took my freedom."

Tamil shifted to his feet. "Why do you want to sit with me?" He had to know. Nothing was ever free.

Riskel shrugged. "It's rude to refuse to eat when you're a guest in someone's home. If we sit together, you can have my plate too, and save me from looking ungrateful."

That made sense. Tamil wasn't sure if it was wishful thinking on his part, but he would sit with Riskel at the next meal and hope for the best.

SHIFTERS SCAR *under the right circumstances.* Those words wouldn't leave Riskel's head. They scarred under the absolute worst of circumstances—if someone purposely disfigured them. The marks on Tamil's wrists looked like bite marks, as if someone fed from him and then poured acid in the wounds to stop them from healing properly. In one meal, Riskel had realized a hundred things about Tamil. Each one broke his heart. He'd watched as Tamil had shoved food in his pockets, obviously expecting to be starved after today. Each time the boy had looked away, Riskel had slipped more food onto his plate, hoping some would find its way inside his mouth.

Tamil had offered his blood as payment. Riskel's gut churned at the idea. Not because Tamil's blood was dirty, as the boy believed, but because he knew biting Tamil would likely break him. That wasn't something Riskel could imagine. As much as he wanted to be angry over Tamil's sneak attack that had left him half dead, he realized now Tamil was an injured animal, lashing out from the pain and starvation.

Riskel hadn't been lying when he'd turned down Tamil's blood. Not only was Tamil malnourished, he was also anemic and suffering from dozens of other ailments that came with severe neglect and abuse. Tamil's blood wouldn't sustain anyone. Not to mention, while feeding, Riskel was vulnerable. Tamil was likely to attack in his panic at the first piercing of his skin. Still, Riskel had considered sipping from him just to wipe away the boy's fear that he was soiled in some way. Everything about this was horrible. Riskel couldn't escape the terrible sensations crawling on his skin. He didn't know if Tamil had any hope, but Jonathan obviously believed. Since Riskel believed in Jonathan, he would try. It wasn't in his nature to turn away from a fellow slave. Maybe the circumstances of their imprisonment weren't the same, but Tamil had been someone's chew toy. Riskel would do what he could.

In the front room, Jonathan sat on the couch with both his men while everyone else milled around, obviously getting restless. If anyone shot Tamil any irritated glances for being forced to wait, he wouldn't have seen them. Tamil never lifted his stare from his feet as he headed for the corner. It was obvious he tried to keep his back safely against the wall while staying out of sight. Riskel followed him and then placed himself bodily between Tamil and the rest of the room. He braced his feet and crossed his arms over his chest, daring anyone to make a move. Riskel wasn't a warrior, but neither was he helpless. He'd been turned vampire by a powerful voodoo priestess. She'd taught him everything she knew. Magic lived in his blood. Riskel would not allow any more harm to come to the boy.

Jonathan eyed him while wearing a knowing smile. Riskel met his eye. Jonathan gave him a subtle nod of approval.

Niall stood. "Since everyone is here, let's talk about our current circumstances. Recently, Jonathan had a vision. Even though it wasn't clear, what has become clear is that danger is definitely headed our way. Two vampire families in the area have already gone missing." That caught Riskel's attention. Jonathan hadn't mentioned that part, only that he'd seen evil in his dreams. "We've extended an invitation to our kin to stay with us, pool our powers and resources to stay safe until we figure this out." He motioned Riskel's way. "Riskel has agreed to remain here until the visions make more sense. His magic could be a huge help. I've also spoken with Baptiste and Eirik, but as long as Tamil is here, they'll not join us."

Riskel glanced over his shoulder, wondering how Tamil took the news.

Tamil seemed to be trying to make himself smaller.

Jonathan spoke up. "Since Tamil isn't going anywhere, they'll either have to get over it or fend for themselves. I think they're capable of holding their own, so I'm not worried about them."

Niall nodded. "I'm not either, but there are weaker vampires who might choose to join us, especially since the disappearances."

Dougal, the blond beauty of the bunch, cursed. "We cannae catch a break. There's always something to fix. Do we at least know what or who we're up against?"

Jonathan took over again. "We can't be a hundred percent certain the missing families didn't willingly leave. The only things I've been able to decipher from the visions so far are it's something old, evil, and burning."

"Burning?" Lire's face screwed up in confusion. "How do you mean burning?"

A small movement behind him caught Riskel's attention. Tamil was shifting from one foot to the other as if frightened and hoping to sneak away.

"Do you know what he speaks of?" Riskel asked quietly over his shoulder, trying not to draw attention to them.

"Pyro," Tamil whispered back. "Demon prince of deception."

"Well, fuck," Lire said, obviously overhearing.

"That explains why there hasn't been a direct attack," Jonathan added. Vampire hearing was obviously on point today. "It also proves I was right to save Tamil. He's already shown himself as useful." To Riskel's amazement, everyone nodded. These men believed in Jonathan. If he said Tamil deserved a chance, they would give him one. Not that Tamil noticed. He was too busy staring at his shoes.

"Well, there's nothing we can do right this second," Niall said, chiming in. "For now, I plan to get some sleep. Later, we can start searching for as much information as we can dig up on this demon. Dougal will take first watch."

"I can add some warding around the property, if you'd like," Riskel offered.

Dougal nodded. "We appreciate the help." With a plan in place, they were set free to do their thing. Riskel chewed his lip as he watched Tamil silently slip away without notice. He let the boy go. Nothing would help Tamil as much as time. For now, Riskel would do his best to keep Tamil safe while he healed.

CHAPTER
TWO

Riskel didn't sleep well. After spending two hours working on wards, he'd fallen into bed half dead. In a matter of minutes, he'd realized no amount of exhaustion would pull him under. The usual sounds of the bayou were missing. It had been years since he'd spent so many nights away from home. He wouldn't have expected to miss his bed so much, but he did. Not to mention the frogs; he missed their constant singing. He rolled onto his side for the thousandth time. His heart leapt into his throat as he realized he wasn't alone.

On the floor, near the door, Tamil slept. There was no blanket or pillow to ease his comfort. On his side, with his hands pillowing his head, Tamil looked uncomfortable and cold on the hardwood floor. Riskel spent a few minutes staring at him. He didn't think he'd slept more than five minutes at a time. Riskel had no idea how long Tamil had been there or how he'd appeared so silently. If nothing else, Riskel would've thought the man's steady heartbeat would've alerted him of his presence.

A smile tugged at Riskel's lips. Two could play this game. Riskel concentrated on the kitchen. The room appeared around him. He dug through the fridge and found some fruit and yogurt as well as some muffins from the pantry. With his arms full, Riskel appeared, hovering over Tamil's sleeping form. He dumped the food beside him and zapped away, reappearing in the bed. For ten minutes, he chewed his lip and stared at the wall. He wondered how long it would take for Tamil to find the food. Giving up, he rolled over. Tamil was gone, so was all the food. He shook his head in amazement.

The next time Riskel slept, he left a pillow on the floor. When he woke, Tamil was back. His head rested upon the pillow, but there was no blanket in sight. Still, a smidgeon of triumph snaked its way in. It was a start. Once again, he raided the fridge for Tamil, and once more, everything including Tamil was gone the next time he looked. He considered setting an alarm at the door, but he didn't want to frighten Tamil or make him think he wasn't welcome.

From the first night, each time he went to bed, Riskel tried a little harder to make Tamil's sleeping arrangements more comfortable. He wasn't sure if Tamil chose his room because he was scared, trying to protect the source of his food, or if it was a reason he hadn't considered. No matter the motivation, he couldn't let Tamil sleep with zero comfort. On top of extra blankets and pillows, Riskel moved the pile a little closer to the bed each night. When Tamil let it go on, Riskel went a step further. He moved to the edge of the bed, leaving the side by the door empty. After zapping home and gathering all the pillows from his house, Riskel built a pillow wall down the center of the bed, clearly marking their separate sides. He didn't expect Tamil to accept right away, but he needed to try to get him off the floor. That wasn't healthy for someone who already suffered enough ailments.

This time, he didn't sleep. A smile pulled at his lips when the bed dipped beside him. Only then did Riskel give himself permission to rest. He knew

Tamil would be gone before he woke, and they'd never speak of this. Riskel was okay with that as long as Tamil stopped sleeping on the hard floor like a dog. Less than an hour later, a blood-curdling scream tore Riskel from a dreamless sleep. Tamil fought an invisible foe. His legs and arms flew in every direction, threatening Riskel's safety.

"Tamil." At his call, there was no response. Tamil was obviously trapped in his head. With no other choice left to him, Riskel pinned the man's arms to his sides and held Tamil against him, refusing to let him get away. Tamil's breaths came out in harsh and rapid pants. There was no way oxygen reached his brain, but he finally settled. He no longer fought what Riskel couldn't see. "Shhh," Riskel soothed against his ear. "I have you. You're safe." Their wall of pillows had disappeared in the fight. Tamil's body shook in Riskel's hold. His teeth chattered.

"You never told me the story about gaining your freedom," Tamil reminded him. The way his voice shook in time with his body left Riskel feeling seasick from the constant movement. Still, he didn't relax his hold. He needed to keep Tamil this side of his nightmares.

Riskel settled down, finding a more comfortable spot without letting Tamil go. His lips brushed Tamil's temple without thought. He needed to bring the man comfort. Something inside him needed Tamil to get better. "A beautiful woman came to me while I slept. I thought she was a dream, but she left me gifts in exchange for sharing my blood. Each day, I woke with something new. A gold piece, exotic fruits, and potions I didn't know existed. Every day, I'd wrap the gift in cloth and hide it beneath the floorboard in my quarters." Riskel spoke softly against Tamil's hair, hoping to soothe him. "One day, another slave saw me hiding my gifts and told on me. He thought I'd been stealing, and we'd all be punished once the goods were missed. My stash was confiscated, and I was beaten until there was no skin left on my back. The pain was unimaginable. It was like being skinned alive with a knife and left for the flies. As I lay there suffering, the beautiful woman with demon eyes appeared. She offered me a trade. My life for my master's riches." There was more to it than that, but Riskel stuck to the highlights. No good came of dredging up the past. "In truth, I was out of my head. I would've agreed to anything to make the pain stop. When she asked for my life, I thought she meant for me to become her slave. It wasn't until it was done I realized I'd agreed to be turned and I'd be bonded to her for life. Nor did I realize my master's riches would come at the cost of me taking his life."

"So you are mated?" Tamil's tone didn't give away his thoughts, but his voice was steady.

Riskel took it as a win. "I was, yes."

"What happened to her?"

"She was killed by a member of Bleidd's pack. Maria wasn't a good person, but she was my mate. That's why Bleidd and I do not get along. He stands by his pack. I must stand by Maria."

"Did you love her?"

Tamil sounded half asleep. That was the only reason Riskel answered. "I was as loyal and obsessed as anyone is with their blood mate."

"Unnatural." The word was slurred.

"Yes," Riskel whispered, hoping not to wake Tamil if he'd finally fallen asleep. "I would not have loved her without that unnatural bond. Not only was I in love with someone else when she turned me, being kept against your will isn't love. It's sickness." Tamil didn't respond. Riskel listened to his heart beat. It was steady. His breathing was deeper than normal. Riskel loosened his grip but didn't release him. He caught himself petting him. Riskel forced his hands still. There was something about Tamil. He couldn't explain why he needed the boy to get better, but it mattered to him. "What nightmares bring you to me every night, sweet one?" He would find out what terrorized Tamil in his sleep, and then he'd do his best to wipe it away. Tamil didn't realize it, but he'd given Riskel purpose. That was something he hadn't experienced in years.

FOR ALMOST AN HOUR, Tamil watched Riskel sleep. He didn't know why it was so fascinating, but it was. Riskel was so still, he almost looked dead. The only difference was the occasional eye movement beneath his lids. He'd always heard that meant someone was dreaming. Tamil wondered what someone strong like Riskel dreamed about. Maybe, like Tamil, he didn't dream but remembered. He doubted Riskel had any memories like his. At least, he hoped the man didn't. Tamil's humanity and sanity had been hacked away bit by bit so many times, he couldn't be fixed. He was certain even his soul was gone. As long as his head and heart were intact, the rest of Tamil would grow back—in theory. It was a theory Draven had tested thoroughly. Tamil had been chopped to bits so many times, there was nothing left of whoever he'd been born to be. Every night, he suffered the punishments over and over again. He wanted to cut them from his brain.

The weeks he'd spent mimicking Riskel, he'd been different. Powerful. Unafraid. Of course, it wasn't really him. He'd only been playacting. Maybe being strong didn't really suit him. He had too much hatred in his heart. Tamil pushed from the bed, moving quietly. He didn't want to disturb Riskel. Tamil was a master at sneaking from room to room. For years, moving quietly was the only way he survived.

There were fresh clothes on his bed when he slipped back inside his bedroom. Tamil assumed Jonathan was the one who kept sneaking new clothes into his room. No matter who was responsible, Tamil couldn't turn down the chance to be clean. He relished taking long, hot showers. No one could understand how much he enjoyed being locked away inside a steam-filled bathroom, free to wash. For years, he'd been scared to remove enough clothes even enough to use the toilet. Tamil's stomach churned at the memory. Still, he found the courage to undress. Of course, he'd also moved a large glass shelf in front of the bathroom door. He hoped if anyone broke down the door, the shelf would give him a little extra time to dress or escape.

Beneath the stream, Tamil closed his eyes. Inside his head, with the hot water streaming down his body, Tamil was transported to a different place. Normally, when he wanted to get away, he made up stories in his mind. Today, Riskel wouldn't leave his head. The moment Tamil closed his eyes, Riskel's gorgeous face and kind eyes appeared. Riskel didn't look at him the way other people did. There was no hatred or pity. He couldn't explain it. The man's stare was something new. Something Tamil had never encountered. The way Riskel had held him when he'd been taken by the memories again wouldn't leave Tamil alone. His skin felt overheated at the thought, and it had nothing to do with his shower.

The heaviness of his cock caught his attention. Tamil dropped his chin and stared down the line of his body. His dick stood, ready. Tamil blinked at his erection in confusion. His cock was obviously stupid. Riskel didn't want him like that. Of course, since Tamil was twisted and broken, it didn't surprise him that the slightest bit of kindness had him ready to drop to his knees. Tamil chewed his bottom lip. Maybe Riskel wouldn't hurt him. Without thought, Tamil stroked himself. His eyes fell closed as the first hint of pleasure sneaked in. The way Riskel held him only hours earlier wouldn't relent. Damn, the man's chest and arms had been solid. He'd smelled good too. Tamil squeezed his cock near the tip as he pumped at his erection. His hips rolled. Impure images rolled through his mind. He tainted Riskel, taking the man in all the ways he'd been taken. He tried to stop as the images turned against him. It was too late. He was too close. His self-control was gone. Tears streamed down his face as jets of cum coated his skin. He swiped at his stomach, trying to wipe it away. The sting it left behind wouldn't abate. He openly sobbed as he scrubbed harder at his skin. It wasn't enough to remove his filth. He didn't deserve to think those things about Riskel. He'd ruined the man's kindness. His brain itched. Desperation and madness owned him. His skin was dirty. He couldn't get clean. The soap and hot water didn't help.

With his mind trapped in a loop of destruction, Tamil's fist shot out. The glass door shattered. He didn't think. Tamil needed out of his skin. He grabbed the first piece of glass he could find and scraped at his skin. The taint wouldn't come off. He was trapped inside this unclean body. He cut away at his forearms and stomach, trying to make the burning stop. He couldn't see through his tears, but he could feel the filth crawling on him.

"Stop. Please stop."

Tamil could hear Riskel begging him, but he couldn't find him. There was too much tainted skin between them.

Riskel's voice got louder. His face cleared. Those whiskey eyes he liked were staring at him with concern. Tamil took a breath. Reality became a little clearer. Riskel's white T-shirt was soaked with blood and water. The material molded to his skin, showing off a washboard stomach. It finally settled into his brain that Riskel was standing inside his shower, holding his wrists and stopping him from tearing at his skin.

"Riskel." Even to his ears, Tamil sounded hoarse.

"I've got you. Please stop."

"You shouldn't touch my skin. It's not clean." Tamil's voice shook.

Riskel pulled him against his chest, uncaring of the blood. "There's nothing wrong with your skin, sweetie. Just stop. I'll fix it. Okay?"

Tamil didn't know how Riskel could fix it, but he believed. "Okay."

"For fuck's sake," Riskel roared, making Tamil jump. "Everyone out. This isn't a fucking show."

Tamil caught sight of several shocked faces as Riskel covered him with a large towel without ever releasing him. Tamil's entire body shook like he'd never be warm again. His mind retreated. He could see everything happening to him, but he felt nothing. It was like it wasn't real. Riskel carried him to the bedroom. He carefully dried Tamil's body, caring for his wounds.

"They're already healing," Riskel said as he wiped away the blood. He piled blankets on top of Tamil until it looked like he was buried beneath a mountain of covers. Still, no warmth settled into his skin. The shaking wouldn't relent. Riskel whipped his shirt over his head and tossed it aside. "I have to try to get you warm. Don't worry. I'll leave some blankets between us. You don't have to worry I'll hurt you." He climbed under the covers with Tamil, doing as he promised. Riskel held him so tight he could barely breathe. Tamil didn't struggle. His fingers brushed through Tamil's hair. The motion confused Tamil as much as it comforted him.

"Riskel."

"You know, my friends call me Risk," Riskel muttered. "I prefer that."

Tamil took a deep breath, forcing his lungs to fill before slowly releasing the air. "Risk. I'm sorry."

Risk took a ragged-sounding breath. "You scare me, because I don't know how to help." The pain in Risk's voice forced more tears from Tamil's eyes. There was nothing he could say. He didn't think he could be helped, and he didn't know why Risk would want to try. Tamil didn't believe he was long for this world. No one could hurt this much and survive.

THREE

Tamil looked so much like an angel while sleeping. It was hard to believe he'd been trying to skin himself alive only minutes earlier. Risk's insides still shook. At first, he hadn't known what was wrong, but something in his gut pulled him toward Tamil's room. Then, he heard the crash. Still, he'd tried knocking. When the darkness pressed hard on his brain and his knocking went unanswered, he'd smashed through the door. Unfortunately, that had drawn a crowd.

As long as he lived, Risk knew he wouldn't forget the sight that met him as he came through that door. It was like Tamil wasn't there. His body had been left empty and set on self-destruct. If he hadn't shown up, how long would it have gone on? How far would Tamil have gone? He'd have to watch him closer.

The bedroom door opened. Risk expected to see Jonathan. Instead, it was Dougal. "You have a visitor." At Dougal's whispered announcement, Riskel checked to make sure Tamil was still sleeping. His heartbeat and breathing were steady. He hated leaving Tamil unattended, but Risk slipped from the bed. "You might consider cleaning up," Dougal suggested as he hit the hallway. Risk glanced down at himself. His jeans were covered in blood and there were spots of dried blood caked on his arms.

"Yeah. I guess so." Even to Risk's ears, his voice sounded dead. He'd never witnessed anything like Tamil's breakdown. Risk was shaken to the core.

"He has demon sickness."

At Dougal's offhand remark, Risk tried shaking off his shock enough to follow. "What?"

"That boy," Dougal said, motioning toward Tamil's room. "It's demon sickness. That's why he can't control it. It's not his fault."

"I know."

Dougal nodded. His blue eyes looked kind. It was obvious he understood Tamil in a way most people wouldn't. "You might not be able to save him. He was held captive for years, tortured in ways you can't fathom. When his first captor tired of him, Tamil was passed on to an even worse nightmare. There might not be enough of his mind left to reach."

In spite of the seriousness of their discussion and in the face of Dougal's dire warning, hope still rose in Risk's chest. "I think he's still in there." He gave Dougal a sharp nod. "Yes. He's still there."

Dougal didn't hesitate, buoying Risk's hope. "Good. You'll make him better. I'll let your guest know you'll meet him out front in a few."

After thanking Dougal, Risk ran to his room to clean up. He didn't think to ask who was there to see him. In fact, he didn't really care. All he wanted was to rush things along and get back to Tamil. He didn't want Tamil to wake up alone. Risk was more than a little surprised to find Saber waiting for him. He liked the man, but they weren't close. Still, Riskel smiled. "Hey, man. It's been a while."

Saber was a Were tiger. He looked like a predator and eyes followed him everywhere. The man had definitely won the gene pool lotto. He smiled brightly at Risk's welcome. "Hey. I thought I'd come rescue you for a little while."

Risk's face screwed up in confusion. "Save me from what?"

"Duty, of course. I brought the bike and an extra helmet if you'd like to get away."

"I'm not really free to leave right now."

Saber's smile fell. Riskel noticed the huge blond didn't look as happy as usual. "Why don't we go outside for a few?" Risk offered, waving him toward the door.

"Yes." Saber brightened. "Less chance of being over heard out there."

Risk thought that was an odd thing to say, but he followed the man outside. It never ceased to amaze him how huge Saber was. His wide shoulders took up too much room, and he towered over everyone. The man's long blond hair flowed down his shoulders. Saber truly was gorgeous. Yet he did nothing for Risk.

Once outside, Saber crammed his hands in his pockets and walked toward a spot in an open field. Risk fell into step beside him. After a few yards, a tingle ran down Risk's spine. He sneaked a look over his shoulder.

"Do you ever make potions?"

"What?" Risk asked, his head whipping back in Saber's direction.

"Potions. Do you ever make them?" Saber looked uncomfortable as fuck. He had Risk's attention.

"Occasionally. Why?"

Saber crowded his space, looking a little too happy with his answer. "What would it take to convince you to make one for me?"

Risk took a step back. The feeling of being watched intensified. He cast a surreptitious look around. A movement beneath a willow tree caught his attention. He could feel Tamil there. He forced his gaze back to Saber. "You don't have to convince me. I'm always willing to help a friend as long it's not something to hurt anyone. But I would've thought Baptiste would've been your first choice. He's older and has a more practiced hand." It took every ounce of his strength not to look Tamil's way. Riskel pretended not to notice the blue eyes like a summer's day following his every move. He didn't want to out the boy in case he was scared of Saber, and that was why he stayed hidden. Even though Risk knew Saber was more tomcat than tiger, he didn't want to draw the man's attention to Tamil either. Risk needed to protect him from Saber's lecherous ways. He couldn't begin to imagine how Tamil would react to Saber's open flirting. The man couldn't help it, but Risk would hate to be forced to break Saber's dick off if he threw Tamil into another panic attack.

"Maybe I hoped to see you," Saber said, swiping his fingers down Risk's chest. "I can't trade favors with Baptiste."

Riskel tried putting some space between them. Saber kept closing the distance. "Um. I'm not hurting for favors. You can pay me back somehow at a later date. Plus, it's not like I could put together anything right now. It'll have to wait until I get home to my stuff."

Saber touched his jaw. His voice turned sultry. "What would it take to convince you to help me tonight?" With each word, he moved a little closer until his lips were barely an inch away.

Risk ducked out of Saber's hold. "I'm currently helping the king. Like I said, if it's an emergency, you should go see Baptiste. If you're willing to wait for me, it won't cost you a thing. I don't mind helping out my friends."

Saber blew out a sigh. His hair flew away from his face on the breath. "It's somewhat personal, so I'd prefer to wait on you. That doesn't make it any less of an emergency. Not to mention, I sort of can't go to Baptiste, because he's kind of the person who cursed me."

Saber looked more genuine than Risk had ever seen him. "Okay," Risk said, dragging out the word. "I have so many questions right now."

Saber ran his hands though his hair, looking frustrated. "So I guess just call me when you're back home."

Risk nodded. "All right. If it looks like it'll be more than a few days, I'll make a special trip out there just to throw something together. Will that work?"

Saber nodded. His smile looked a bit strained. "I appreciate it." Risk realized Saber didn't look so great. There were lines around his eyes and dark circles under his eyes.

"It'll be okay," Risk promised. "There's a counter spell for every spell. I'll make sure you're fixed."

Saber slapped his shoulder. "I really appreciate it, man. This has been a huge nightmare. I'll let you get back to our king. Whatever he has you working on has to be more important than my issues. Plus, you know, the faster you're done..."

"It was good to see you."

Saber winked and headed back toward the house. Risk waited until he was out of sight before heading to the willow tree where Tamil hid. Risk ducked beneath the curtain of hanging branches. Tamil sat crossed legged on the grass beneath the tree. He smiled at Risk. The gesture took Risk's breath. He had dimples.

"You knew I was here."

Risk dropped onto his side next to Tamil. He dug his elbow into the grass and propped his head up. "I spotted you as you were crawling under here." Risk plucked a long weed growing nearby and twirled it between his fingers.

Tamil scratched the bridge of his nose and stared at something in the distance. "Is that guy who you're in a sexual relationship with?"

Tamil's inquiry caught Riskel off guard. If he hadn't already been on the ground, he might've fallen. Tamil's questions were always incredibly straightforward. Risk wasn't sure Tamil knew how to beat around the bush. "No. Saber is only a friend. In truth, I'm not even sure we're very good friends. It's more like we hang out in the same circles."

"He tried to kiss you," Tamil pointed out while still not meeting his gaze.

"Yes. He tried. I wasn't interested." Without thought, Risk trailed the long piece of grass down Tamil's arm. He watched as chill bumps rose on his skin.

Otherwise, Tamil didn't acknowledge the move. "People confuse me."

"Me too," Riskel admitted with a chuckle. A shy smile flashed his way. Risk couldn't stop staring. "We should talk about something better than confusing men. What's your happiest memory?" He thought Tamil could use some happy talk.

A line appeared between Tamil's eyebrows. "I don't have any happy memories."

"Not a single one?" Riskel couldn't hide his disbelief. "What about when you were little?"

Tamil shook his head. "I can't remember that far back. The earliest I remember is my parents dying. Even then, it's more like I recall the emotion and not the details. Like, I remember being scared and alone. I had a hard time controlling my powers, so I kept changing forms. When I saw a wolf, I became one. That's when Bleidd took me in, but the moment he realized I wasn't a wolf, he put me right back out. Then, there was nothing but fear and pain." Tamil tore off a blade of grass and tossed it.

Risk couldn't imagine the hell Tamil suffered, but he could change things now. "Today is a new day. What would you like to do? I'll help you make your first happy memory. Is there any place you'd like to go? I'll take you."

"I'm a prisoner here. You shouldn't take me anywhere." Tamil didn't sound upset, only resigned.

"You're not in a prison. Think of it more as a resting place. You're taking a break. I'm sure if you'd like to go somewhere, Jonathan would let me take you."

Tamil shook his head. "There's no place I can think of going. I'm not unhappy right here."

Risk couldn't let up. "There has to be more you want than this. Come on. Confess one wish."

A blush touched Tamil's cheeks. His gaze slid Risk's way before moving away as quickly. "Um." He scratched the bridge of his nose again, looking nervous. "I've never kissed anyone in this form. Would it be okay if I kissed you?"

Even though he was slightly taken aback, Risk tried not to show it. "You want to kiss me?"

Tamil nodded.

"Okay." At his answer, Tamil finally looked his way, as if shocked Risk would agree. "But," Risk added, needing to set some ground rules. "You have to promise me that you'll stop if you panic or feel uncomfortable. Don't try pushing through. This is supposed to be a happy memory. Deal?"

"I promise."

Since he had Tamil's word, Risk held still and waited. It twisted his heart how uncomfortable

Tamil looked. Tamil leaned his way. Risk fought the urge to meet him halfway. This had to be all Tamil. Their lips brushed. Risk's skin tightened. Tamil smelled sweet—like something from a dream Risk couldn't quite place. The kiss went from innocent to burning in an instant. Tamil's lips parted. His tongue swiped Risk's bottom lip. Risk found himself opening. Their tongues met. Risk lost his breath. It didn't matter they didn't touch in any other way. Risk's body was on fire. He'd never wanted anyone as quickly. But he wouldn't touch Tamil. It was possible any move in that direction might send him spiraling out of control again.

Tamil pulled back. Risk opened his eyes and his gaze landed on a stranger. All innocence was gone. Tamil's stare was hungry and deadly. For a moment, Risk wondered if he was about to get fucked or murdered. Tamil was terrifying, and yet Risk couldn't stop. There was a madness inside him when it came to Tamil. If the boy needed Risk to die to reclaim his life, Risk would freely give it.

"I'm sorry." Even Risk didn't understand why he apologized. "I have to know," he added as his hand ran up Tamil's arm, moving toward his neck until he gently cupped the back of Tamil's head. "I have to know," he repeated as he urged Tamil's mouth back to his. This time, as their lips met, Risk tumbled backward. Tamil's upper body covered his. To his surprise, not only did Tamil not balk, he didn't panic. He kissed Risk like he felt something too.

"What do you have to know?" Tamil asked as he pulled away. He settled down with his ear pressed to Risk's chest, as if he listened to Risk's heartbeat.

Risk's fingers found Tamil's hair. He brushed through the soft locks. "Why I feel closer to you than I do anyone else," Risk answered honestly. Tamil's gaze was so trusting, it was humbling.

"Did you figure it out?" Tamil kept his voice low, as if afraid to break their spell.

Risk didn't know how to respond. In short, yes, he very much feared he knew the answer, but there was nothing uncomplicated about it.

"I feel close to you too," Tamil said when Risk couldn't find his voice.

Yes. Risk knew that too. In spite of all his mental damage, Tamil wasn't completely broken. The part of him that still clung to humanity would recognize Risk. After all, Goddess Celeste was never subtle when she fated mates. Fuck his life. He wasn't sure he could do this. As he stared at Tamil, he knew he'd kill anyone who tried harming him again.

It was possible Tamil should move away, but Risk hadn't balked, and his heartbeat was so soothing. Plus, Risk kept brushing a long piece of grass down Tamil's arm. Even though it tickled, he didn't want it to stop. They'd kissed. That reality kept sneaking its way in too. Not only had Risk let Tamil kiss him, he'd kissed Tamil back. There was this odd tugging in his chest. He wanted to cling to Risk like a needy child in hopes the sensation never stopped.

"There you are."

Tamil tore his gaze away from Risk's gorgeous eyes and focused on Jonathan as the man crawled beneath the curtain of branches.

"Hey," Risk said in way of greeting. Tamil flashed Jonathan a small smile. He wanted to be aggravated over having his peace interrupted, but it was Jonathan. Jonathan was incapable of disturbing peace.

"This is my favorite tree too," Jonathan said as he plopped down in the grass beside them. "So, whatcha doing?"

"Making a happy memory." Tamil marveled over the lack of shame in Risk's response. Even though Tamil was a criminal and had attacked him, Risk wasn't ashamed to be with him now. It was humbling.

Jonathan nodded. "This is a great place for that. You know, we once had our annual orgy under this tree."

Tamil sat up. Now it was uncomfortable.

Jonathan snorted. "I'm joking." He glanced behind him. "I'm pretty sure we were closer to the house."

A rumble of laughter escaped Risk, leaving Tamil confused. He wasn't good at telling if someone was joking. But he loved the sound of Risk's laugh.

Jonathan's expression turned serious. "I thought we'd try healing you a little more today. If you want to go inside, we can."

Tamil shook his head and went back to lounging on Risk's chest and staring at the man's eyes. "This is a good spot."

Jonathan glowed brighter, so much so Tamil saw it happen from the corner of his eye. "I'm sorry, sweetie," Jonathan said, rubbing Tamil's ankle. "You'll have to give me a bad memory so I can find the poison in your blood."

Tamil nodded, enjoying the way Risk's shirt felt against his cheek. "I used to change my feet," Tamil said, picking a memory that was bad but not unbearable. "It was such a small thing, but I knew they weren't mine. When I felt helpless, I would stare at the feet that were nothing like my own and pretend I was someone else. Someplace else. I don't know how I was found out. He had an uncanny way of stripping away everything. Instead of forbidding me from changing, he waited until he caught me at it." Tamil closed his eyes because he couldn't watch Risk as he said the words. "He sawed off my feet as punishment. It was the first time I'd endured that."

The heat from where Jonathan touched his ankle increased. He could feel the hurt separating from the memory, stripping away the pain. He could look at the moment and not feel the horror. Tamil sighed in relief. Exhaustion washed over him. Everything went dark. There was nothing but peace.

FOUR

A SPELL CHANTED THROUGH RISK'S MIND AS HE weaved the material into a doll. She would be strong when he finished. It gave him something to do while Tamil slept. He'd carried the man inside the house after Jonathan worked his magic. Tamil hadn't budged at all since. Risk took up a spot on the couch and waited. His nerves were on edge.

Jonathan appeared over his shoulder. "A poppet. That's a great idea."

Risk shrugged. "I thought any amount of healing and protection from evil I can give Tamil is better than doing nothing." For fuck's sake, they'd sawed off a child's feet. Risk stopped breathing every time he thought about it.

Jonathan sat on the floor at his feet and watched him work. "The last time I did this, Tamil slept for two days. It might do him some good if he does so again." It seemed odd to have a man more powerful than a god keeping him company. Risk had so many questions and Jonathan had the power to answer every one, but Risk couldn't find his tongue. Jonathan wasn't intimidating. Risk just didn't know where to begin. It was the same as standing in front of Goddess Celeste herself where all life's many questions could be answered. There was too much to ask, so he asked nothing at all.

Instead, Jonathan ended up being the one with a question. "Do you understand what you're getting yourself into?"

A snort escaped Risk. "No. I have no clue what I'm doing, but I'm doing it anyway."

"He's your blood mate," Jonathan said quietly, as if he said it too loud the words would set off a grenade. "I guess you've probably figured that out."

He'd known, but hearing Jonathan say it made it real. Risk's chest expanded as he took a deep breath. "Yes." And there was nothing he could do but make a protection spell and watch his mate suffer. "He's a shape shifter. I didn't realize that was possible, but here we are."

Jonathan nodded. "He can be anything, even a vampire. I'm assuming that was Celeste's reasoning when she chose him for you." He paused for a minute. When Jonathan spoke again, he sounded unsure of how he'd be received. "You could go back to your life out in the bayou and hide from this, you know. I don't think anyone would blame you."

"I'd blame me," Risk said, setting the doll aside to focus on Jonathan. "I would always know that Celeste handpicked someone for me, and I left him to suffer alone."

To Risk's surprise, Jonathan swiped at his eyes, as if fighting off tears. "I'm not sure how much of his damage I can fix." It sounded as if the confession pained Jonathan, but he didn't stop. "Dougal spent a few months with Lire without any protection from demon exposure and he has permanent damage from that small amount of time. And that was with Lire treating him well." Jonathan looked grim. "Tamil spent years with a demon, being endlessly tortured in ways that would destroy a person without the poison of a demon's touch."

Risk was hooked. Jonathan knew everything. He wanted to know too. "I admit I don't know much about demons. Maria ensured our land was protected from them and we didn't travel often. The one time we left the country, she was killed, so that didn't inspire me to leave my little haven again after that."

"When I was first turned, I thought of everything in our world as magical," Jonathan said, as if admitting a dirty secret. "I thought vampires could hear thoughts because fairies existed—like things didn't have to make sense any longer, but really, everything has a reason. Almost a science to it. Think of the poison dart frog. It's poisonous because of its diet. Lust demons need lust to survive. Pride needs pride. Deception feeds on..." Jonathan's eyes lost focus for a moment before he made a dismissive sound. "Anyhow, demons aren't always evil, especially if they're not raised to be, but most are raised that way. Mostly, because they stick to their own kind and never learn a new life, but they kind of have to stick to their own because they're poisonous —literally. Depending on their classification, they each excrete a different type of venom like most people have oil on their skin. Lire is a lust demon.

Touching his skin without protection would make you crazed with desire. Kallus is a product of pride. His touch would drive you mad with always trying to be the best at everything. You'd be an over-achiever to the extreme—like severely manic. You see what I mean?"

Risk nodded. He was intrigued.

Jonathan continued. "It's a sickness—like having the flu, except worse. On top of feeling horrible, you have the side effects that come along with whatever demon you've been exposed to. The longer the direct contact, the worse the sickness. For Tamil, he was held by a deception demon. It's like having your mind eaten away. Every good thought constantly undermined. A bad person could be deceived into thinking they're good, which would be bad for everyone else—like creating the next Hitler. But an innocent child like Tamil, I can't imagine. Every good thought turned bad. The things he loved turned nightmare. Can you imagine what you'd do to get away from your mind if there was nothing good at all?"

Risk's stomach churned, and his eyes burned. He couldn't get the image of Tamil in the shower out of his head. "You'd try to skin yourself alive in the shower."

Jonathan nodded. "Exactly, and I can eventually leach away the poison from his blood, but he'll never be completely fixed. The damage is already done. It won't be enough to love him, Risk. You'll have to love him for the both of you, because he'll never love himself."

Defeat weighed on Risk's shoulders. He didn't know if he was strong enough for this.

Jonathan smiled, as if he heard Risk's thoughts. "The good news is, he could love you enough for the both of you, and love is always the answer to everything. It's the strongest magic in the world." Jonathan nodded toward the poppet. "You should weave some into that doll. That way Tamil feels you even when you're not around."

"I like you a lot," Risk said without thought.

Jonathan didn't give him time to be embarrassed by the confession. "Ditto. You're a good man, but FYI, you should let Saber stew a little while. He's being taught a life lesson right now."

"Yeah, what's up with that?" Risk asked, thankful for the subject change. Everything had been all stress for so long his brain needed a break. Saber was the perfect topic for senselessness. "He was pretty desperate earlier. I've never seen him scrambling for help like that."

Jonathan snorted. "Baptiste made him believe he's impotent. I made it true." Jonathan released a loud cackle as he made the confession. He covered his mouth as if trying to hold in the sound.

Risk couldn't stop smiling. "That's mean. Funny, but mean."

"Meh," Jonathan said with a shrug. "It's only temporary. His dick could use the break. Plus, he's being set up for something greater in life. Also, he did something mean to Evan, and that's like kicking puppies."

"Really? That is like kicking puppies." As he said the words, he remembered the man he was fated to love had kidnapped Evan. Threatened him. His smile fell.

Jonathan shook his head. "Don't do that. It wasn't him. Not really. The more time he spends free of the demon's touch, the closer he gets to being himself again. The real Tamil is in there, and he'd never hurt anyone. I will say this, though," Jonathan said, turning serious. "Tamil is powerful. Even more powerful than anyone knows. That's why he draws evil to him. That's also why you wouldn't have healed without my help after he attacked you. Shapeshifters are a rarity on their own, but Tamil is also half mage. He was never taught to control his magic, but that doesn't make him any less dangerous in the wrong hands. Pyro will never stop coming for him. That's why we have to stop him before he gets to Tamil again."

Risk's mind screeched to a halt. "Wait. You mean to tell me this demon you've been seeing is after Tamil? The same demon who held him captive?"

Jonathan nodded. His guilty expression said it all. "I'm sorry. He doesn't know we know, and I'd like to keep that way. For his sanity's sake. Don't worry. We'll keep him safe, but we need him to get better, because he's likely the only one who truly knows how to find this demon. Pyro is a demon prince, which we've dealt with before, but only that one time. Tamil got free of this somehow and from somewhere without any help. We need to know how and where. No pressure," Jonathan added with a humorless laugh.

So much for giving his mind a rest. Now not only did Risk have to figure out how to make someone love him who would never love himself, he also had to pry the man's worst memory from him. Great. No pressure was right.

———

TAMIL OPENED his eyes and his gaze landed on a doll. An unexpected smile pulled at his lips. He tugged her closer, almost afraid to show his pleasure. So far, in this house, no one took things from him if he liked them, but that fear was still real. There was a vibe pulsing from the doll he couldn't resist. She smelled familiar. He eyed her blue dress and white bandage face. She was plain but powerful.

"Do you like her?"

Tamil's gaze shot to the side of the bed. Risk sat in a chair next to him with his feet propped on the bed. Tamil clutched the doll to his chest and inhaled. "I feel her magic."

Risk dropped his feet to the floor and sat forward. "She's a protection poppet. With some other things added in," he added. "She'll keep you safe as long as you have her with you."

Tamil's eyes stung. "Thank you."

Risk treated the gift as if it was an everyday occurrence. "What would you like to do today?" As if plotting against him, Tamil's stomach growled. A bright smile lit Risk's face. "Breakfast it is. You go take a shower and I'll raid the fridge."

His mind got the best of him. He eyed the bathroom door with fear. The last time he'd taken a shower, it hadn't gone well. Still, his lips moved with no thought from his brain. "Okay."

Risk's gaze moved to the door as well. "The shower door has been replaced. Do you want me to go with you?"

Gah, he felt like a five-year-old. "No. I'm fine." It was a complete lie, but whatever. It wasn't the first time he'd tried sawing off his skin and probably wouldn't be the last. He'd survive.

"All right. I'll find food." Risk sounded so damn sure Tamil would be okay it was hard not to believe. Still, the moment Risk was gone, Tamil sneaked the poppet into the bathroom too. She would keep him safe. He could feel her strength. Tamil rushed through his shower and morning routine while trying not to catch sight of his reflection. After he dressed, he hid the poppet beneath his shirt and headed back out to the bedroom. Tamil couldn't explain his actions. The doll felt good—like happiness was wrapped inside. He didn't want to put her down. Risk was back, but there was no food.

He smiled as his gaze landed on Tamil—like he was happy to see him. The thought did something to his chest. Risk stood. "I went to get you something to eat but was told you are missed and the guys would like you to eat at the table with them."

Tamil blinked. "Why would I be missed?"

"You've been asleep for two days. They were worried."

"Oh."

"So will you join them?" Risk looked so hopeful Tamil couldn't say no.

"Yes." Even Tamil heard the uncertainty in his voice, but he still headed for the door.

Risk eyed him, making Tamil realize he still clutched the poppet beneath his shirt. Even though Tamil was embarrassed, he couldn't put it down. Risk closed the distance between them. "Come here, sweets. Let's do this," Risk said, lifting Tamil's shirt. He used part of the poppet's dress to tie the tiny doll to the belt loop of Tamil's jeans. "There. Now she can stay with you and you won't have to worry about losing her."

"Thank you." The words clogged in Tamil's throat. He couldn't stop staring at Risk. He had kind eyes.

Risk stepped closer. He brushed his fingers along Tamil's jaw. "You don't have to thank me. Not ever. Okay?"

Risk's shirt twisted in Tamil's hands, making him realize he held it. Even once he noticed, Tamil didn't release him. "I don't deserve for you to be nice to me."

Risk's smile took his breath. "I think you deserve the world."

He'd never wanted to make anyone proud before. In that moment, Tamil was determined to try harder than he ever had to reclaim his life. "I guess we'd better go eat." Even as he made the claim, Tamil didn't release Risk's shirt.

"In a second," Risk said, shuffling closer. The moment Risk dipped his head, Tamil met him halfway. Their lips barely brushed, but they lingered. Tamil's heart skipped a beat. He never wanted to let go. Having someone want to kiss him so sweetly was a new feeling that he couldn't stop wanting to hang on to. This house. This man. It was all temporary. Soon enough, evil would win. Evil always won. Tamil would be back in hell, bound and broken. He wasn't sure yet if this moment would sustain him or kill him when that day came.

VAMPIRISM MEANT life kept odd hours. Risk had turned at the age of nineteen in 1849. In over one hundred and fifty years of breakfast being at night, Risk still had days when it felt odd. Today was definitely one of those days. While Tamil ate, and Risk sneaked more food onto his plate, the rest of the guys planned a party. It seemed it had been deemed a day of rest.

Even though Tamil still kept to himself, he'd stopped sitting away from the group. He appeared more than a little fascinated by watching Faolan. The ginger of the group had legs like tree trunks. He was seriously huge. Risk had no problem seeing him tossing houses or whatever it was they did in the Scottish games. Even knowing Faolan could break him in half didn't stop Risk's jealousy from growing. It was ridiculous. Tamil needed to come out of his shell. Risk was used to having all Tamil's attention. He tried not to care. It was like the harder he concentrated on everyone else at the table, the harder his jealousy churned. Having an unclaimed mate was hell on the mind.

Despite his best efforts, Risk's gaze slid Tamil's way again. He was still staring at Faolan. But now there was a line between his eyes, as if he fought himself. Risk couldn't look away.

"That magic will die."

The room fell silent. Every head turned Tamil's way. He immediately withdrew. His life force turned inward, and it could be felt like oxygen being sucked from the room. Risk tried not to panic, but Tamil's instant fear choked him.

Faolan's expression turned kind. "It's okay, boy. Don't be afraid to speak up. You have to in this noisy crowd."

Tamil glanced up from beneath his lashes. When he obviously could find no fault in Faolan, he reached out and touched the leather bracelet tied around the man's wrist. "That won't last forever." With his gaze locked on Faolan's wrist, he twisted the bracelet, running his finger along it as he went. "It's already weakened here." He turned it a little farther. "And here."

Dougal stood and moved to Tamil's side. He dropped to his haunches. "What of this one?" he asked, holding out his arm and revealing a similar bracelet. Judging by his panic, Risk assumed they were important.

Tamil gave his a similar inspection. "It's holding up, except for this one spot," he said, tapping a frayed spot. "This isn't a permanent solution."

"But Baptiste said Jonathan's hair couldn't be broken."

Tamil shook his head at Dougal's words. "It's not the hair that's fraying. It's the magic. Baptiste is powerful, but he isn't powerful enough to create a permanent spell."

"Is there a permanent solution?" Dougal asked. The way he stared at Tamil made the hair stand on the back of Risk's neck. His muscles tensed. Jonathan set his hand on his thigh beneath the table, calming him.

Tamil's gaze moved to Lire. He nodded. Tamil stood. As he moved to Lire's side of the table, he wrung his hands. Risk ground his back teeth. Trepidation filled him to the point of breaking. Tamil looked ready to bolt or crumble. Until that moment, Risk hadn't considered what it cost Tamil to sit at the same table as a demon.

Tamil's hand shook, but he held it out to Lire.

Lire made no move to take it. "I can't touch you."

Tamil shook all over but didn't relent. "You won't hurt me."

"No," Lire said, sounding firm. "I'm the seventh son of Asmodeus. Any contact with me would break you."

"There is *nothing* you can do to me." Tamil's voice was hard, but it was nothing compared to his eyes. The stranger was back. "Take my hand."

Lire cast a desperate look Jonathan's way.

Jonathan nodded. "I think you should listen."

Lire's chest expanded on a deep breath. He stared at Tamil's outstretched hand and finally accepted.

Risk held his breath.

If Tamil was affected by Lire's powers, he didn't show it. "Your men will have to drink from me."

Risk tried to intervene again. Jonathan kept him in place.

Even as Tamil held his free arm out, he didn't look Faolan's or Dougal's way. He kept his face averted. Risk couldn't tear his gaze from Tamil. He was so brave. So much braver than he got credit for being. He had more strength than everyone at the table combined. The difference was no one present had endured his pain.

"Please hurry," Tamil begged in a hoarse whisper.

Faolan and Dougal exchanged glances. "At the same time to make it faster?"

Dougal nodded at Faolan's suggestion. They each took Tamil's arm, and side by side, they bit. The most heartbreaking whimper Risk had ever heard escaped Tamil. Risk's eyes fell closed. Jonathan's grip tightened on his thigh. Tears pressed against his eyelids, burning for release. He'd never felt more helpless. Jonathan released him as Faolan and Dougal retracted their fangs. He jumped to his feet and was at Tamil's side in enough time to catch him as he collapsed. The man's body shook so hard it rattled Risk's teeth.

Tamil tried to speak even as he gasped for air. Risk dipped his head, trying to hear. "I want a happy memory."

"Did it work?" Cin asked, obviously breaking under the pressure.

Dougal unwound his bracelet and touched Lire's face. He did it quickly, as if expecting the worst. "Holy shit. It worked."

Faolan unwound his bracelet and joined in. All three men were smiling like idiots. Risk didn't stick around to see more. He held Tamil to his chest and headed for the back door. His steps didn't slow until he ducked beneath the branches of the willow. With his back to the trunk, Risk sat with Tamil clutched to his chest. His mind whirled. Jonathan had said Tamil was powerful. This went beyond that. He'd touched Lire with no real repercussions. It didn't make sense when he'd been so tainted by a different demon.

Risk's gaze dropped to the man in his arms. Tamil's eyes were locked on him—like a lifeline. Risk found himself stroking Tamil's cheek. His skin was soft. He looked and felt so fragile. Yet Risk knew it wasn't true. He was battle weary.

"You are the most beautiful soldier I've ever seen."

Tamil blinked as if Risk's voice pulled him from wherever his mind had gone. "I don't look at myself."

Risk hadn't expected the confession. "You should. I think if you really looked, you'd see the same amazingly strong and unbelievably gorgeous person I do."

A tear slid down Tamil's cheek. "I think that's what I'm looking at right now. How can you stand to be near me at all? I hurt you."

A smile pulled at Risk's lips. "It's like it never happened."

Tamil's teeth chattered. "I've done a lot of terrible things."

Risk nodded. "Me too."

"Do you think Goddess Celeste sees me at all?"

"You're in her grandson's home, so I'd say she more than sees you."

Tamil dipped his chin in a sharp nod and closed his eyes. "It's so cold here. It's nothing like this in Hell."

Everything inside Risk froze. He was certain he'd heard right, which meant... a thousand things, and none of them were good. There was a very real possibility Tamil had given him the answer Jonathan was looking for. If so, they were so fucked.

CHAPTER
FIVE

Risk had no idea how much time passed while he held Tamil. He watched as the guys started a bonfire nearby. Tamil's shaking stopped. He could've been sleeping or unconscious. All Risk knew was his heartbeat was steady, and he felt right in Risk's arms. Lire appeared beneath the branches, saving Risk from his ever-growing silent desperation. The demon's long dark hair hung in his face, making it hard for Risk to tell his mood. He nodded toward Tamil. "Is he okay?"

Risk eyed Tamil, looking for any lingering signs of distress before meeting Lire's gaze again. "He's strong. This will pass."

Lire sat, looking unsure of his welcome. "How did he do it?"

With a shake of his head, Risk tried coming up with any explanation, but he knew there was nothing. Tamil was one surprise after another. Since setting eyes on him, Risk hadn't understood anything. "I don't know."

"Deception," Tamil muttered, sounding half asleep. Riskel glanced down. Tamil stared up at him. "Nothing kills lust like deceit. When you touched me, your gift mixed with the demon sickness I already carry. Your men drank my tainted blood. It'll do permanent damage before it clears their system. Now they can touch you. I became like a living shot of immunization."

Lire chewed his bottom lip. He didn't look anywhere near as happy as he should. "What does that do to you?"

Tamil sat up. "Nothing that hasn't been done before."

"We never would've asked that of you, but thank you."

Tamil didn't look directly at Lire. Instead, he plucked at the grass. "You love each other," he said with a shrug. "People only use me for bad things. This one time, it wasn't."

Risk had to look away.

Lire didn't back down. "You're allowed to say no," Lire said, sounding firm. "In this house, no matter the circumstances, you can say no. No one here would ever hurt you or choose their happiness over your wellbeing. If you can't say no, but you feel it, find me. I will say no for you, okay? You are not alone."

Risk had never been prouder to know anyone than he was the people in this house. Lire's blood mates were his life, but still he chose to protect the mental health of someone the rest of the world would shun.

Tamil nodded.

Risk couldn't stop himself from brushing the back of his knuckles down Tamil's cheek, bringing the man's gaze from the ground to him. When he had Tamil's attention, Risk smiled. Tamil always looked so trusting when he looked at Risk. "Are you okay?"

"Yes." It was the smallest whisper.

"Are you ready to join everyone? It looks like they're dragging out the speakers. I imagine our ears are about to be assaulted by some crazy Scottish fire dance shit."

Tamil smiled. "I've never seen that."

"You should definitely join us then," Lire said, sounding cheerful. "We're fully committed to embarrassing ourselves tonight."

"Yes. I'll come."

"Awesome," Lire said, backing out from the branches.

Risk shifted to his knees, determined to do the same. Tamil flattened his palm on his chest, stopping him. "You're allowed to tell me no too. If you don't want to stay here, I'll understand. You don't have to take care of me, even though I appreciate it."

"I want to be with you," Risk said, shuffling forward. Before he could think too much about it, he pressed a quick kiss on Tamil's cheek. Tamil turned his head before he could move away. Their lips met. Tamil clutched Risk's head and held on. He deepened their kiss, stealing Risk's breath. In the blink of an eye, the moment had gone from a quick kiss to heated. Risk

74

knew he'd be hiding an erection when he crawled from their hiding spot. Tamil's teeth sank into his bottom lip and a pant escaped Risk.

"Come on, guys," Jonathan called, cutting through his growing lust.

Risk leaned away and met Tamil's gaze. He looked every bit as turned on as Risk felt. Risk couldn't resist touching Tamil's kiss-swollen lips. His chest felt heavy. "There's nowhere else I'd rather be." Risk moved away before he lost himself any more than he already had. As it was, nothing would ever be the same.

FROM HIS SPOT on the bed, Tamil watched Risk get ready to go out. He could feel Risk's hunger. Risk needed to hunt. To feed. It hurt and confused Tamil. He didn't understand why it bothered him. It was a ridiculous way to feel. His unrealistic anger was the same as if Risk got mad for Tamil eating dinner. Even as fucked in the head as Tamil was, he understood that was nonsense. Still, the pressure sitting on his chest wouldn't abate.

Risk froze as he pulled a T-shirt over his head. His gaze swung Tamil's way. "Stop."

Tamil automatically dropped his gaze to his lap. "I'm sorry."

Risk closed the distance between them and sat on the bed next to Tamil's thigh. He gently touched Tamil's chin and urged him to meet Risk's gaze. "I meant stop being mad at me. Your anger is clawing at my brain."

A lump rose in Tamil's throat. He didn't want to be this way. "Ignore me. I'm being stupid."

"Your feelings are never stupid. Maybe you should try talking to me instead. You never know. I might understand."

A loud huff escaped Tamil before he could stop it. "I don't even understand myself." He hated pouting like a child. His emotions were all over the board. Even though he'd given up all pretense of sneaking into Risk's room and simply went to bed with him each night, Risk didn't belong to him. They weren't lovers. He couldn't tell the man his fangs belonged to him. Tamil's insides froze at the thought. Did he really feel that way? Fuck. Yes, he did. Tamil swiped his palms down his thighs. He was such an idiot. Risk still stared at him—expectant. "Um." He cleared his throat. "It's... I just... ugh. I'm being ridiculous and even I know it, but I don't really want you to bite anyone else." He sneaked a peek at Risk as he made the claim. To his surprise, Risk didn't laugh.

He rubbed Tamil's thigh, as if trying to comfort him. "If I don't feed, I'll die."

"I know," Tamil said with a sharp nod. "That's why you need to go and not worry about me. I can feel your hunger. It's an ache in my chest."

Risk didn't move. Instead, he continued trying to ease Tamil. "And what happens when I get back? You won't feel better. I don't want you to be upset with me."

This was hell. He knew Risk was right. All the pep talks in the world weren't stopping him from feeling cheated. It didn't matter it was ridiculous. Risk's fears were legitimate. He wasn't sure he wouldn't break down once it was done. Tamil hated himself more than usual in that moment. Risk was so good to him all the time. All Tamil did was weigh him down with neediness.

"I'll go to my room," Tamil heard himself say as if the offer came from someone else. He squared his shoulders. Tonight, he wouldn't be weak. "That way, I won't know. I'll just see you tomorrow, and you'll be fed. We can act like nothing happened."

"Is that what you want?"

"No." The truth spilled from him without any thought.

Risk looked too damn understanding. He didn't know how to lie to the man. "What do you want?"

"To be normal," Tamil cried, sounding angry even to his ears. "I want to be fucking normal, so you can come to me when you need blood. You have no idea how much I hate this. I hate being trapped inside this." He motioned toward himself, feeling helpless.

To his surprise, Risk never flinched away from his rage. He simply nodded as if every hate-filled word leaving Tamil's lips was justified. "I want it to be you too." At Risk's confession, every ounce of anger and jealousy bled from Tamil. He held his breath. "If I could choose, I'd always pick you." There was no subterfuge in Risk's voice. He meant it. "It's very hard for me to control myself with you, especially when I'm hungry. I'd never want to hurt you. But yeah, I want you."

Tamil swallowed. "Would you kiss me before you go?"

"If you're okay with that, then yes."

He couldn't stop. "Will you kiss me when you get back?" The hunger flashing in Risk's eyes made Tamil bold.

"If you'll let me, yes."

Tamil licked his lips, feeling his nervousness grow. "Will you promise not to do more than bite whoever it is?" He shook his head. "Never mind. I don't have a right to ask that."

"You're the only one who has the right," Risk said, bringing Tamil's hand to his mouth. His warm lips brushed Tamil's skin. Every nerve in Tamil's body sang. He didn't let himself think. Instead, he snagged the collar of Risk's shirt and hauled him closer. As their lips met, he shifted onto his knees and pushed, taking Risk to the mattress. Even though he knew Risk was stronger than him, the way Risk let him be in control always made him feel powerful. His heart and body knew he belonged with Risk. It was only his fucked-up brain that got in the way. If he could turn it off, everything else always clicked. The way he felt when their tongues stroked helped steal his traitorous thoughts. Risk was hard for him. He could feel the man's erection searching for him. The feeling of being unstoppable grew.

His lips moved from Risk's mouth to his jaw. He needed to taste the man's skin. When he reached Risk's throat, he sucked. A soft moan vibrated from Risk's chest. Tamil's heart squeezed. He loved that sound. It was beautiful—like he was good. Like he made Risk happy.

"You'd better go while you still can."

Risk nodded, even as he tried reclaiming Tamil's lips. "Come with me."

Tamil leaned away. Lust made his thoughts hazy. "What?"

"Come with me," Risk repeated. "Watch it happen. That way, you'll know I only want you."

"Okay." The word barely passed Tamil's lips before the air shifted and Tamil found himself standing in a dark alley. Soft Jazz music floated from a distance. Street lights barely did their job a few streets over. A man pushing a bike headed down the alley. Risk stepped into his path. The man startled, but the moment he spotted Risk, he went still—like falling into a trance. Risk didn't go for the man's neck, but still, Tamil couldn't look away. As Risk brought the man's wrist to his lips, he met Tamil's gaze. Tamil could see Risk as clearly as if they stood in the daylight. His whiskey-colored stare was for Tamil. His emotions were only for Tamil. The instant Risk's fangs pierced the man's skin, Tamil pressed his hand to his stomach. There was no jealousy—like he'd feared. Instead, his already skyrocketing desire doubled.

It was over as fast as it started. Risk's fingers encircled Tamil's wrist. His gaze never wavered from Tamil's. They were connected in a way he couldn't understand. He didn't want it to end. The bedroom reappeared around him. Risk walked backward until he reached the edge of the bed. He sat and tugged Tamil forward until he stood between Risk's knees. Risk's fingers found the knot in Tamil's pajama pants. He tugged. His gaze moved upward. Tamil looked into the face of his other half. The good half. He trusted him with everything. Risk pushed Tamil's shirt higher, exposing the skin above his waistband.

As Tamil watched, Riskel's tongue shot out, brushing his bare skin. Tamil locked his knees when they weakened.

No one had ever touched him like this. He kept holding his breath, expecting Risk would stop any moment and never touch him again. Instead, Risk's fingers curled around the edges of Tamil's pants. He dragged them down, freeing Tamil's erection. Tamil wanted to shy away. His body wouldn't budge. All he could do was watch as Risk's tongue swiped his crown. His fingers found Risk's shoulders. He held tight as Risk's mouth opened. Tamil caught a glimpse of the tips of Risk's fangs before he swallowed Tamil's cock. A sharp breath caught in Tamil's throat, choking him. Part of him wanted to beg Risk to stop. He didn't want his cum in Risk's mouth. The sight of Risk sucking his cock was fascinating. It felt amazing, but the vision he presented was what Tamil couldn't get past. Risk's jaw flexed. Tamil wanted to feel it beneath his fingertips. He found himself stroking Risk's face, living in every second of the moment. Risk looked like he loved what he was doing. He made Tamil want to love it too. His eyelids were heavy with desire. They tried falling closed. Tamil forced himself to watch. He might not ever get this again. This was one more happy memory no one could take.

Every muscle in his body tensed. Tamil craved the release. He couldn't come in Risk's mouth. Panic rose even as the pressure beating at his crown increased. There was a voice screaming in his head for him to push Risk away before he poisoned him with his evil. His body wouldn't budge. The suction on his cock was too tempting. Risk's lust-filled expression held him captive. The first wave of ecstasy hit. A cry left his lips. Risk kept sucking, taking him down his throat. Tamil's knees gave out, but Risk held him in place, dragging every twinge of pleasure from Tamil.

Tamil bit the inside of his cheek so hard he tasted blood. Terror owned him. His cum was inside Risk. He wanted to tear it out. "Shhh," Risk soothed against his stomach, as if he felt the fear paralyzing Tamil. "Come here," Risk said, dragging Tamil into the bed and rolling him beneath his weight. Being pinned beneath Risk should've sent him into a frenzy of panic. Instead, it was comforting, especially once Risk's lips skimmed his cheek. "It's okay. You did it, baby," Risk whispered against his ear. "You're so strong." He could feel Risk's erection pressing against him, and he didn't feel strong. Tamil felt like a failure. He hadn't pleased Risk. Even though he hadn't freaked out over Risk feeding from someone else, he hadn't fed him. He'd left the man unfulfilled. "You have no idea how special you are to me." Tamil's eyes fell closed at Risk's claim. His chest hurt. Risk deserved so much more.

Tamil dug beneath the blankets and found his poppet. With his fingers wrapped around her for strength, he turned his head and captured Risk's lips. It was the hardest thing he'd ever done. He could taste his cum on Risk's tongue and his insides churned like acid ate at his guts. Then, something else happened too. His heart slowed. The panic died away. Risk's sexy flavor overpowered everything else. He could breathe.

His teeth found Risk's bottom lip. He tugged and sucked, loving the way Risk's mouth felt against his. Without thought, he urged Risk out of his shirt. Risk had the best stomach. It was hard with rippled muscles that still managed to somehow feel soft beneath Tamil's fingertips. His shirt irritated his skin. It kept Tamil from feeling that amazing stomach against his. With an aggravated growl,

Tamil ripped off his shirt and tossed it aside before reclaiming Risk's mouth.

"I could kiss you forever," Tamil confessed in a whisper against Risk's lips. He needed Risk to know how much he meant.

Risk's hips rolled. His hard dick ground against Tamil's body. "I'm sorry." Risk tried rolling to the side as he made the apology. Tamil held tight, refusing to let him go. The way Risk felt pressed against him was heaven. He wished Risk could climb beneath his skin to get an inch closer. His body itched with greed. He found his fingers digging into Risk's back, trying to drag him closer.

"Don't stop," Tamil begged. "Not yet."

At his plea, Risk deepened their kiss. His hips rolled again. This time, he rolled away before Tamil could stop him. "I'm sorry," he breathed, sucking air. "You're too tempting. Just give me a second to cool down."

Tamil rolled to his side and used Risk's chest as a pillow. He listened to Risk's heart race as he stared down the line of his body. There was an obvious bulge in Risk's jeans. It seemed so odd to Tamil that he could make Risk hard. Him. Someone with nothing to offer.

With no real plan in mind, Tamil's hand slid down Risk's body. He needed to feel Risk's erection. Risk sucked in an audible breath as Tamil's hand swiped over the bulge in his jeans. An unexpected wave of power surged inside him. He'd done that. Tamil wasn't alone in his feelings. It might only be lust, but Risk felt something for him too. He popped the button on Risk's jeans.

"You don't—"

"Shhh," Tamil soothed against Risk's chest, cutting him off. He slipped his hand inside Risk's jeans. His fingers shaped Risk's erection. The man's crown was soaked. Tamil's stomach muscles tensed. It was incredibly sexy, knowing he was the reason Risk was this turned on. He tilted his chin up and met Risk's gaze. His hooded expression made Tamil's mouth water. He stroked Risk's cock, loving how soft his skin felt. Tamil kept his touch light so he didn't scare Risk away. He expected to get shot down any second. Tamil didn't want to stop. He liked the way Risk watched him. Tamil found himself opening Risk's pants wider, giving him more freedom to explore. He dipped lower, running his fingers through Risk's pubic hair. It felt rough. Tamil couldn't stop touching him. He'd never wanted to do this to anyone. Tamil had been forced to do a lot of things. This was the first time he wanted it. He went back to exploring Risk's cock. It was long and thick. His crown looked wide. Tamil toyed with the slit, watching as pre-cum leaked out. He smeared the juices with his fingertip, wetting Risk's crown. It was oddly satisfying. Tamil was lost in his discovery. He sat up and urged Risk out of his jeans. Risk quietly allowed Tamil to do as he pleased.

Without an ounce of shame, Tamil moved to sit between Risk's legs. He'd never had or wanted this much freedom. Tamil took note of Risk's every reaction. If he liked something, Tamil filed it away for later. Risk seemed to enjoy Tamil touching him between his balls and his asshole. He massaged the spot, fighting a smile when Risk squirmed. Tamil moved lower, shamelessly circling Risk's asshole. A soft moan sounded from deep inside Risk's chest, fascinating Tamil. He grew bolder with Risk's every reaction. The tip of his finger slipped inside Risk. Risk made a sound that made Tamil's stomach growl. He'd never been this hungry for anyone.

Risk's cock jumped. More pre-cum coated his stomach. Tamil massaged it, trying to soothe him even as he kept playing with his ass. Risk visibly fought for air. He writhed, as if trying to be still but incapable of doing so. Tamil pumped faster, hoping to unhinge him. He wanted to see Risk lose control. Plus, he loved watching Risk's dick move in his hand. Risk's entire body stiffened. A cry tore from his throat. Jets of cum coated his stomach and chest. Tamil couldn't stop staring or pumping, trying for every drop. It was fascinating and satisfying in a way he couldn't describe.

As Tamil watched Risk come unglued in his hands, he made the biggest discovery of his life. He wasn't strong in the way that got most people through the day, but he was still strong enough to make this amazing man happy, and he would, because Tamil loved him. His eyes burned at the realization. For the first time in his life, he thought it was possible someone might love him too.

CHAPTER
SIX

AFTER THE FIFTH TIME THE DOORBELL RANG, Jonathan shuffled its way, muttering to himself. They still hadn't developed a hard and fast rule for answering the door in a timely manner. Jonathan was certain it shouldn't involve being dragged from bed while others were awake somewhere in the house.

"I mean, it's not that damn hard. Just turn the knob. It's no fucking wonder people pop in and set off the alarm, because no goddamn body knows how to answer the door."

He threw the door open, already irritated.

"I'd like to go on the record as saying I don't want to be here."

Jonathan stared at the group standing on his porch. Baptiste, Kallus, Eirik, Bleidd, and Evan all stood side by side. Even though Baptiste was the one who'd spoken, everyone else was nodding along, except Evan.

"Well, then, don't let the door hit you." He started to close it in their faces.

Evan threw his hand up stopping the door from closing. "I do want to be here. Everyone else is here because—apparently—I'm incapable of coming alone."

Bleidd stroked his back. "Baby, no one said that. We're just looking out for you."

Evan rolled his eyes.

Jonathan was fascinated. "I don't know why you'd care if he came alone. He's been here dozens of times without an entourage escorting him." Still, he made no move to invite them in. He didn't like Baptiste's defiant air. It didn't bode well.

"You weren't harboring a criminal then," Baptiste spat.

Jonathan sighed and pointed at himself. "King." Once again, he tried closing the door on them.

Evan stopped him again. "Please, Jonathan. You once told me that anyone with a good heart is welcome here. I'd like to see Tamil."

Everyone behind Evan groaned. Jonathan's eyebrows rose. "Why?"

"Because I know you wouldn't let him stay if you didn't know something we don't. This is how evil divides us, and I don't like it." He looked sad. That plucked at Jonathan's heartstrings. "I want to come and see everyone, but these guys won't let me until we get this worked out." Oh, the guilt. Evan was too sweet. Jonathan couldn't withstand it.

Thankfully, Faolan appeared behind him, saving Jonathan from being the bad guy. "I say let them in, as long as they understand that Tamil is under our protection and the penalty for harming him is death, then they're golden."

"That's it. We're going," Baptiste said, trying to drag Evan away.

He refused to budge. "We understand. No one will hurt him." Another loud groan went up around him.

Evan's face hardened. "No one will hurt him. Understood?" he repeated. A general rumbling of begrudged agreement surrounded Evan. His smile returned. "See? We'll behave."

Jonathan wasn't so sure, but he still let them inside. "Please, come in. I just woke up, so I have no idea who is where and doing what."

"Everyone is in the kitchen, teaching Tamil how to cook," Faolan said, sounding cheerful and obviously uncaring of any discord.

Jonathan pasted on a smile. "There you go." He headed that way with what felt like an army at his back. Thankfully, their kitchen was huge. They'd built the house with one of the main focuses being on eating meals together. The kitchen and dining room were one gigantic room. One half was nothing but a long table that would seat up to eighteen people. Yet every grown man in the house was huddled around the stove.

Jonathan picked a chair at the table and sat. Eirik and Kallus did too, as if they had no real skin in this game. Bleidd and Baptiste hovered as Evan joined everyone else at the stove.

"Oooh, add chocolate to that pot and peanut butter to the other," Lire said, sounding like a little kid as he directed Tamil.

Tamil did as told. Jonathan smiled at the sight. "This is good, right? I don't know what I'm doing."

"It smells good," Evan said, dragging all eyes his way, except Tamil's. He automatically withdrew into himself. His head bowed. Risk molded against his back, hiding him from sight.

"Hey, Evan," Lire said, sounding cheerful. "We haven't seen you around in forever. I thought you'd come for the full moon."

He nodded, not backing down and making Jonathan proud. "I wanted to come, but you know..."

"Do you mind finishing this?" Even though Tamil whispered, Jonathan heard him clearly. He imagined everyone in the room did.

"Hi, Tamil," Evan said, sounding nervous. "I don't think we've formally met."

Everyone watched the exchange with bated breath. Tamil lifted his chin long enough to flash Evan a sweet smile before retreating again. Jonathan swore the circle around Tamil tightened. Even though no one was showing their unease, Jonathan could feel the tension like a physical thing.

Evan didn't back down. "I know it's a lot to ask, but would you mind stepping outside with me for a minute?"

Tamil nodded and headed for the door. Evan fell into step behind him. A group of overly large Scots blocked the way before anyone else could follow.

"They'll be fine," Niall said, herding everyone toward the table. "The worst that'll happen is Evan will sweet talk him to death, or Tamil will cry and melt him. Everyone find a damn chair and sit."

Jonathan glanced around the table at the sea of nervous faces and shook his head. It was like no one believed in him any longer.

RISK LOOKED around at the people gathered at the table. Everyone was visibly trying to hide their thoughts. Risk busied himself trying to read everyone. His mind needed anything to do other than think of Tamil and Evan alone. He wasn't worried about Tamil hurting Evan or vice versa. Risk was worried something would set Tamil off and he'd break down while Risk wasn't there to help. Cin looked bored. He kept tilting his chin to the ceiling as if looking for cracks. Niall was obviously pissed off that no one seemed to trust Jonathan's assurances everything would be fine. He was glowering at everyone at the table. Jonathan seemed to feel the same. Lire, Faolan, and Dougal were switching their gazes between each other, as if having a mental discussion about who would be the first to break Niall's order to leave Tamil and Evan in peace. Eirik, Kallus, and Baptiste were trying a little harder to hide the fact they were having a similar discussion while Bleidd traded glances with Risk. They were the ones whose hearts were outside.

Lire swept his fingers through Dougal's hair. It was the first move anyone made. All eyes turned their way.

Baptiste sat forward in his seat. "How are you doing that?"

Dougal blinked. "What?"

He waved his finger between Lire, Dougal, and Faolan. "You're touching each other without the bracelets I made for you. How are you doing that?"

"Tamil found a way," Dougal said, keeping his voice level.

Baptiste didn't let up. "Such a thing isn't possible. Magic like that doesn't exist. How did he do it? *Why* did he do it? You had the bracelets I made. Don't you realize this is probably a trick?" The more Baptiste spoke, the more his temper rose with each word.

Luckily, Lire kept his calm. "The bracelets you made were weakening."

"Not possible," Baptiste said before Lire could answer his other questions. "I've had the necklace Celeste made for years without any problems. Those bracelets were made recently. They shouldn't be weakened."

Niall motioned Faolan from the table. "Go get one. Let Baptiste take a look."

With a nod, Faolan disappeared and immediately reappeared, holding one of the leather bracelets. He handed it to Baptiste. Baptiste eyed the piece carefully, feeling of each stitch. "Dear Goddess. It's frayed in spots. You can't tell unless you really look, but it's there."

"Tamil could tell by sitting close to it," Risk said, incapable of staying quiet any longer while Tamil's motives were being questioned.

Baptiste handed the bracelet back. "Still, Tamil isn't to be trusted. If he's found a way to avoid needing a talisman, I wouldn't put my faith in it being a permanent fix. It could fail at any moment, leaving you exposed."

"It's not a trick," Jonathan said, putting an end to the discussion. "His fix is real and solid."

"How?" Baptiste said, sounding hard.

When Lire spoke, he sounded even harder. "At great sacrifice to himself, that's how."

Baptiste sat back. His expression screamed disbelief, as if he'd been betrayed by his closest friends. "I don't understand any of you. This man kidnapped Evan, threatening him with the worst and most vile things. He attacked you, Risk, leaving you for dead and taking over your identity. Yet all of you have taken him in and obviously opened your home. He isn't a prisoner here. You're treating him like an honored guest. He does one spell to help you and you turn on us."

Jonathan slammed his hand on the table, bringing all eyes to him and making Baptiste fall silent. "Enough. I know this is not who you are," Jonathan spat, eyeing Baptiste with open anger. "You have a good heart. Use it to see this man. He deserves a chance. We are extending that same chance to Bleidd, who has also shown he can be cold and dangerous."

Bleidd sat up straight. He looked like he couldn't believe he'd been dragged into things. "Me? What did I do?"

"You turned out Evan, leaving him alone and exposed to... well, I'd say God only knows what, but we do know, don't we? After all, you'd already done the same to Tamil when he was only *ten years old*." Jonathan emphasized Tamil's age, ensuring Bleidd heard the sin for what it was.

"He was hurting other wolves, younger wolves."

"Because he couldn't control magic he didn't have anyone to show him how to use it," Jonathan shot back. "You don't turn a child out into the cold. For god's sake, you find someone who can help them and turn them over to the proper people. You don't abandon them in the woods for a fucking child predator to find." By the time Jonathan finished, his eyes swirled with melting gold and he'd grown a foot. He was terrifying.

Bleidd deflated. "I made a mistake."

"That's more than a mistake, Bleidd. It's a criminal offense in the human world." Jonathan shook his head as if he couldn't believe he was having to explain such a thing. "I get that your world is different and that you've had to make choices as a pack leader that I don't envy. I'm also not blind to the fact that Tamil wasn't the typical child. He has abilities beyond what most people can handle or understand. That's why you're still sitting at my table and not roasting in a pile of ash. But, honestly, I'm not happy with any of you," Jonathan said, eyeing everyone except his mates since they seemed to be the only ones immune from his ire.

"Damn," Faolan said, sounding confused. "What did we do?"

"You don't trust me," Jonathan spat. "I've said they'll be fine alone, but you don't believe in me. I see you." He eyed each of them individually. "All the way to your souls," he added. "I know your good traits and your hidden secrets. You can't hide anything from me. Tamil and Evan, they are no different. They are not immune to my abilities. Both men are so pure at heart it would blind you to see their souls." Jonathan switched his gaze between each person, as if ensuring they understood how serious he was, before focusing solely on Baptiste. "Evan makes it easy, because life hasn't tainted him. He got lucky. When Bleidd turned him out, Celeste found him. He was allowed to keep his innocence and purity. When you look at him, you can see how sweet life has allowed him to be. Tamil wasn't lucky."

Jonathan visibly swallowed and shook his head. "He wasn't lucky," he repeated, sounding broken. He cleared his throat. "But his soul, they didn't break that. At his core, where I can see, he is Evan's twin. His heart is so beautiful, kind, and innocent. It breaks me to think of how cruel you'd like to be to him when he has endured so much unspeakable horror. You should be ashamed." Jonathan sat back and swiped at his eyes like he was barely holding his shit together. "Risk. Bleidd. Go be with your mates. They are fine, but you're obviously not."

Risk and Bleidd exchanged a glance before pushing to their feet. Risk headed for the door but paused when he reached Jonathan's side. He squeezed his shoulder. *I believe in you.*

I know.

Risk squeezed him once more at the mental reassurance. Jonathan was right to think Risk needed to get to Tamil. The separation was killing him, but not because he was alone with Evan. But because he hadn't claimed Tamil yet. Every day, that knowledge grew like a tumor inside him. Tamil was his. The longer he waited, the worse the ache would get. Claiming him meant a blood exchange. That was something he wasn't sure Tamil's mind could take.

"So Tamil is your mate," Bleidd said the moment they stepped outside. He sounded every bit as uncomfortable as Risk felt.

Risk didn't look his way. "Yes."

"That's good."

Even though Risk wasn't sure if Bleidd meant it, he still nodded, because it was good. In fact, it was amazing. If he could ever claim him, that was. Otherwise, it was horrible. When Tamil and Evan came into sight, Risk bit back a chuckle. Beneath a tall tree, Evan jumped up and down, obviously trying to reach a higher branch with each leap. He talked a million miles a minute, making Risk wonder how Tamil kept up. Yet Tamil sat on the ground, smiling and nodding as if he understood every word.

"What are we missing?" Risk asked, moving to join them. He pulled Tamil to his feet and sat before tugging Tamil into his lap. Tamil settled in as if he knew where he belonged.

"Evan caught Baptiste's shop on fire."

"It was a pretty spectacular explosion," Bleidd said, dropping to the ground and adding his two cents to the topic. "It would've taken out half the building if Baptiste hadn't been there."

Evan nodded. "It was bad. I probably won't get to try making new potions again for a while. He was pretty upset."

Bleidd shook his head. "Not about the shop. It scared him that you could've been hurt."

Evan shifted from foot to foot, looking nervous. Risk's heart went out to him. He was sweet and stuck in the middle. "I want to be able to visit again. Without everyone having to tag along," he tacked on.

Tamil dropped his gaze to his lap and twisted the poppet hidden beneath his shirt. Risk brushed his lips across the back of Tamil's neck, trying to comfort him. Tamil snuggled closer to his chest. "I'm sorry about what I did. There's no reason for you to believe me, but I wouldn't have hurt you. I just..." He took a quick breath. It sounded loud—like it hurt.

"You had the demon sickness," Evan said. Understanding laced every word.

"And that's my fault," Bleidd said, cutting in. "You are very powerful, Tamil. I hope that you find someone to teach you to control it."

Tamil never looked up from his lap. "I don't use magic anymore. Not for anything. Not since... not anymore."

Risk tightened his hold on Tamil. It took every ounce of his self-control not to intervene.

"I want to visit you again," Evan repeated, sounding firmer, as if daring anyone to counter his decision.

Tamil nodded. He rubbed Risk's knee, as if searching for comfort. "I want you to visit again too."

"That's fine," Baptiste said, appearing behind them. He sat next to Risk. Close enough their thighs almost touched. He focused on Tamil, even though Tamil kept his gaze locked on his poppet. "Can I ask a favor, Tamil?"

At his question, Tamil cast a quick glance his way. "Yes."

Baptiste tugged a necklace over his head and passed it over. "Would you check this for any weakness?"

Tamil accepted the necklace without meeting Baptiste's gaze. He ran every inch through his thumb and forefinger before passing it back. "It was created by a Goddess. You don't have to worry it'll ever break."

With a nod, Baptiste tugged the necklace back on. "Thank you." He tapped his fingers on his thigh, looking nervous. Risk couldn't stop brushing his lips along Tamil's neck in his own show of nerves. Baptiste cleared his throat. "So, um, I was thinking—if Risk is willing to bring you to my shop—maybe I could help you learn how to use your magic while I'm teaching Evan."

Evan perked up. He bounced. "Oh, yes. Please? I promise I won't blow anything else up if you come."

A snort escaped Baptiste. "You'd better promise that whether he agrees or not."

"Of course," Evan said, nodding. "But, still, please say yes."

Risk's mind whirled. He'd left the safety of the king's property with Tamil to feed. It had been a quick trip. One Jonathan had known about and been watchful for his immediate return. With Pyro on the loose and no real info, Risk didn't know how to respond.

"Why don't we do it here?" Evan suggested before Risk had time to panic. "That way, Tamil doesn't have to leave his newfound comfort before he's ready, and Bleidd and I can run the property while we're here."

Baptiste nodded. "That's fine with me, if it's okay with Jonathan, and Tamil is interested."

Tamil toyed with his poppet's dress. "If Jonathan says it's okay, then yes."

"May I see that?" Baptiste asked, motioning toward the doll Tamil held.

Risk could feel Tamil's hesitation like it was a living thing. Still, after a moment of hesitation, he handed it over. He immediately linked his fingers through Risk's, as if he needed something with so many people watching him. Baptiste brought the doll close to his face and inspected it, making Risk nervous. Old druid magic ran through Baptiste's veins. Any poppet he made would probably put Risk's crude attempts to shame. He hoped he hadn't failed in some way.

Baptiste smiled. "You can tell she was designed by your fated mate." Risk's heart skipped a beat. They hadn't talked about it and he didn't know how Tamil would react. Baptiste didn't let up. "There's so much love inside this charm, she practically vibrates. She's strong." He handed the doll back to Tamil. "She'll keep you safe from most anything."

Tamil tucked her back under his shirt as if he feared someone else would take her. Risk wrapped his arms around him, lending his strength, silently letting Tamil know no one would be taking anything from him. Tamil melted against his chest. His gaze locked on Evan. "You should run the property while you're here. It's not a full moon, but it's still nice. Plus, I made candy. It's probably awful, but..."

"Yeah, there's no more candy," Dougal said behind them, sounding like his mouth was full. "You have to be fast around here."

There's candy. I hid some for you already.

"I knew you would," Tamil said, answering his mental assurance aloud. It had been a test. Tamil had heard his thoughts. Risk's hold tightened on him even more. He wasn't sure Tamil even realized he'd heard the words in his head and not with his ears. But for Risk, it was another sign. He'd have to claim Tamil soon. Otherwise, staying apart would turn mentally painful. Damn, he had no clue what he was doing.

CHAPTER
SEVEN

Tamil decided to do his final session with Jonathan alone. He was no longer passing out while Jonathan cleaned his blood, but Tamil was having to dig deeper for worse and worse memories. That meant delving into things about himself he didn't want to share with Risk. It wasn't that he thought Risk would hate him. Tamil knew Risk would look at him differently. He didn't want to be pitied. Tamil already felt like he wasn't good enough for Risk. Having Risk know those things, he couldn't do it.

Afterward, Tamil went in search of Risk.

Risk was nowhere to be seen, but the bathroom light was on. Tamil twisted the hem of his shirt between his hands as he shuffled closer. Before he made it inside the open doorway, he spotted Risk sitting in the tub. His head was resting on the edge and his eyes were closed. Tamil moved to his knees and slipped inside the room. His motions were silent as always. Risk didn't budge as Tamil settled in, watching him. Steam rose around him. His dark skin glowed with moisture. Tamil barely blinked. He didn't want to miss a second.

"You're the quietest person I know."

A smile pulled at Tamil's lips at getting busted spying. "Obviously not quiet enough."

Risk turned his head. The unnatural glow of his eyes twisted Tamil's gut. "I can hear your heartbeat."

Tamil wondered what it sounded like. If it beat out Risk's name. "Jonathan says my blood is officially clean. Does it smell different?"

Wicked intent flashed in Risk's eyes. "I don't know. You'll have to move closer."

"It wasn't my intention to bother you."

The way Risk watched him made it hard for Tamil to breathe. "You're not."

"You're beautiful." The words were out there before Tamil thought twice. Risk probably heard that all the time. Tamil wasn't special. He didn't have pretty words.

Risk sat up. His gaze never wavered from Tamil. "What would it take to convince you to join me?"

A nervous flutter beat at his belly. He licked his lips. "Just ask."

"Please?"

Tamil came to his feet and crossed the room. Risk's expression turned hungrier by the second. When he reached the edge of the tub, he almost lost his nerve. He sat. Risk ran a wet finger down his arm. Tamil watched in fascination.

"It's okay if you've changed your mind."

Instead of admitting he was nervous, Tamil attacked another issue. "You're hungry."

Risk smiled and settled back against the edge again. "Yes. Unfortunately, I'll have to hunt again later."

"Maybe, don't." Tamil didn't want to back down when it came to Risk. He trailed his fingers across

the water, testing the temperature. "I'd like to try."
Tamil stood.

Risk's gaze followed his every move. "What would
you like to try?"

Tamil took off his shirt as he answered. He didn't
want to see Risk's reaction. If he did, and Risk looked
disgusted, Tamil might never get the courage again.
Still, he swallowed hard, trying to push the words past
his tight throat. "You're my blood mate." He knew it
in his heart. Tamil didn't understand why Goddess
Celeste had chosen him for this amazing man after all
the horrible things he'd done, but she had. She
believed he could do this. He had to believe too.

Risk sat up again and took his hand, dragging Tamil's
gaze his way. "Talk to me." He looked so understanding.

"I want you to try to drink from me." Risk's expression let him know he'd made the right choice. Now
he couldn't stop. "And I want to drink from you."

Risk stood. Water splashed over the edge of the tub.
Tamil found himself hauled against Risk's chest,
water soaking him as Risk climbed from the tub. He

was swept into the tide of Risk. Risk kept moving, leaving Tamil no other choice but to wrap his arms and legs around Risk. In a flash, Tamil found himself beneath Risk. Water dripped from Risk and onto the mattress. Even in his most intense moments, Risk never harmed Tamil or scared him.

"Are you sure?"

Tamil nodded. "You're mine. I feel you every second of the day. I have to try."

Risk's expression kept fear at bay. He looked capable of taking care of Tamil, even at his weakest. "You'll be safe. It won't hurt."

Tamil wasn't sure if that was true, but he trusted Risk. "Okay."

Instead of going for the bite, Risk popped the button on Tamil's jeans. Tamil let it happen. He was willing to let this go wherever it went. Risk's expression was sexy as sin as he peeled off Tamil's clothes. Once they were equally nude, Risk didn't cover him with his body. He kissed Tamil's knee. A chuckle escaped Tamil at the odd move.

"I think about kissing this knee a lot."

"Um, okay," Tamil said, trying not to laugh.

"It's gorgeous," Risk said, sounding serious. "Almost as sexy as this one," he said, kissing the other knee. His lips lingered. Tamil stared down the line of his body, fighting to catch his breath. The vision Risk presented was pure sexiness. His dark, wide shoulders reflected the light as he bent over Tamil's body. His gaze shifted, meeting Tamil's as his lips moved higher. Tamil's breath caught at the back of his throat. His already hard cock twitched. Risk's mouth moved to Tamil's inner thigh. "Of course, I think about this spot too." It tickled as Risk's lips brushed his skin with each word. He fought to stay still.

Risk moved higher, spreading Tamil's thighs wider as he went. His mouth opened over the inside of Tamil's thigh, right next to where Tamil ached for more. He sucked. Tamil's hips left the bed. Risk held him in place. His tongue stroked Tamil's skin, tickling him. Tamil dug his fingers into Risk's shoulders. He wasn't sure if he wanted to pull him closer or push him away. Risk sucked again. A moan escaped Tamil. Pre-cum leaked onto his stomach. Risk struck without warning. His fangs pierced Tamil's skin. Tamil came apart. He'd never experienced anything like it. With each pull of his blood into Risk's mouth, another wave of pleasure rocked him. Without warning, cum hit his chest, making him realize he'd orgasmed—hard. Jet after jet coated his skin. His body twitched with pleasure and the need for more.

Risk crawled up his body. Their skin melded as their lips met. Risk's hard dick slipped through the cum. Their erections met. Tamil was still every bit as hard and horny as if he'd never come. His skin crawled with desire. Risk moved against him, massaging Tamil's cock with his hard dick. They felt amazing together. Tamil couldn't focus on anything other than their erections sliding against one another.

Risk tilted his chin up and sucked air. Tamil stared at him—transfixed. The way his lips parted as he openly sought release held Tamil's attention. His fangs peeked out. With his eyes closed, Risk gave Tamil the freedom to stare until his eyes itched. He could feel Risk getting closer. They were more connected now, but not completely. Still, as Risk's motions became frantic, Tamil struggled too. He reached for more, needing Risk's hot cum on his cock. Risk bit his bottom lip. His face was hard as he pumped against Tamil, making love to him in a way no one had ever touched Tamil. Blood rolled from Risk's lip as his fang pierced his own skin. Tamil shot forward and captured Risk's bottom lip, sucking it into his mouth. Risk's blood filled his mouth. Tamil swallowed. Something tugged at his heart—like shoestrings pulling tight, tying him to Risk. A moan reverberated throughout the room. Cum filled the space between them. Their tongues fought, battling to touch. They were one soul now, stitched together by a power greater than them. Tamil's eyes filled with tears. He prayed he hadn't just ruined a good man.

RISK LISTENED to Tamil's heartbeat as he held the man against his chest. He knew he wasn't sleeping. Tamil stroked his arm, making his eyes heavy. It was too early for bed. Sunrise was a few hours away. Still, he didn't want to move. This was his mate. It was official. Things would never be the same again. His chest felt full. Tamil had been so damn brave during Risk's bite. He'd hoped by choosing a place with no scars, he'd chosen a spot with no bad memories attached. Their mating needed to be a happy memory to build a life upon. The moment felt intimate. It made Risk want to know everything about Tamil, even the parts Tamil didn't want to share.

"Have you really been to Hell? I don't mean metaphorically. You said something that makes me wonder if you've actually been there. Have you?"

Tamil's fingers fell still. "Yes."

At Tamil's answer, Risk's eyes fell closed. He swallowed. The last thing Risk wanted was to ruin their moment, but Jonathan needed answers. Risk thought maybe he did too. He sure as shit didn't want to bring this up again. Once was enough. "How did that happen? If you don't want to tell me, it's okay," Risk rushed to add. "You're mine now. I'll always keep you safe."

Tamil cleared his throat. With his back pressed to Risk's chest and the dark surrounding them, the moment felt like the right one. "You should know. It's only fair. Just promise you won't think too badly of me."

Risk didn't hesitate. "Honest to God, Tam. I don't think you could do anything to make me think badly of you."

Tamil rolled over. His gaze shone in the dark. Risk couldn't look away. "After Bleidd tossed me out, a vampire named Draven found me. He was as evil

116

and sadistic as they come. When I was thirteen, I'd passed the age of interest to him, so he traded me to a demon." It was too late to beg Tamil to stop, but he wanted to. Only Goddess Celeste knew how badly he didn't want to put Tamil through this. He felt Tamil shrug. "Extremely long story short, this demon lived in Hell, so I did too."

"How did you survive?"

"I'm not sure I did." Tamil's answer broke his heart.

Fuck, he really didn't want to keep pushing. "I guess, what I mean is, how did you get out?"

He felt Tamil shrug again, and he knew he'd gotten all he would out of Tamil on the subject. To his mind, it was enough. It was someplace for Jonathan to start. No matter how much the Hellish clan needed the information, Risk wouldn't keep pushing Tamil. It wasn't fair for them to ask for more. At some point, they had to stop victimizing him, so he could start over. Risk wanted that beginning now. He still had to let Jonathan know what he'd learned.

Jonathan. He wasn't sure if the man could hear him or how far away he was, but Risk had to try. He also tried pushing his thoughts from his mind on a different level than he'd done with Tamil earlier. Risk hoped he wasn't overheard. He felt oddly like he was betraying his mate. Risk told himself he wouldn't hide, though. If Tamil learned of Risk and Jonathan's discussion, he'd be honest.

What's wrong? Even Jonathan's thoughts sounded panicked over being contacted this way.

We need a family meeting. I know why you can't find the demon. He held his breath and waited.

Let me know when Tamil is sleeping. I'll call the others.

With a plan in place, Risk turned his attention to Tamil. "I'm glad you got out," Risk said, letting Tamil know he wouldn't push anymore. "Being here with you, it's the greatest thing that's ever happened to me." He couldn't stop the confessions once they started. "Before you, my life was split between being controlled by other people or being trapped in my loneliness. I don't think you realize how much meeting you has given me. You're my personal miracle."

Tamil sniffed. "You're the only good thing." That was it. Tamil didn't expound before capturing Risk's lips. Their kiss was sweet. Risk couldn't get enough of touching and kissing Tamil. He hadn't been simply spouting bullshit. Before Tamil, Risk had been lonely to his core, incapable of settling or bothering to look for anyone. It was almost as if he'd known Tamil would eventually find him, and he hadn't wanted to be busy when he did. Now they were together. Jonathan was right. Risk would love him enough for them both. It was easier than he ever imagined.

CHAPTER
EIGHT

THERE WAS ONLY A WHISPER OF MOTION AS RISK
tried sneaking away. Tamil kept still, doing his best
not to give away the fact that he was awake. It was a
learned skill. Years of mid-sleep attacks had taught
him to play at being asleep like a pro. He could feel
Risk's gaze upon him, checking his vitals. Tamil
didn't peek open his eyes until he was certain Risk
was gone from the room. Even then, he waited,
counting to ten in his head before slipping from the
bed. At the door, he listened, measuring footsteps.
Risk turned left at the end of the hall. Tamil heard it
happen. He followed, staying silent and keeping his
distance. Risk had heard his heart beating in the
bathroom earlier. He kept that in mind as he
followed Risk now. It wasn't like he didn't know

where he was going. He'd heard the man call out to Jonathan earlier. Tamil wasn't upset. If they'd asked him sooner, he would've told them what they wanted to know. He understood they didn't want to upset him. Still, if they were discussing him, he deserved to be included.

By the time he made it to a spot where he could see everyone and overhear their conversation, he'd already missed part of it. He was surprised by the number of people in the room. It was like everyone had shown up for this meeting. Even Baptiste's crew was there.

"Are we talking actual Hell?" Cin asked. They were the first clear words Tamil caught. "Like, Hell? Fire and eternal damnation. Burning alive. The whole shebang?" Cin might've gone on all day if Jonathan hadn't made a dismissive motion, cutting him off.

"We get it. Is that what he meant?" Jonathan asked.

Risk nodded. "The actual place."

Lire chuckled. "Why are you so surprised, Cin? Where do you think I came from? Or Kallus," he added, motioning toward Kallus.

Cin waved off Lire's question. "I get that, but I mean is there a hatch or a door? Are people really traveling freely to and from this place?"

Jonathan cut in. "Niall has been to Heaven. He went in alive and came out alive, so it being possible isn't the problem here. I think we're missing the biggest issue on the plate. We already know there's a key to the heavens. A living, breathing key. It stands to reason there would also be a living, breathing key to the underworld." Jonathan paused and shook his head. "Guys, if so, that means Tamil has seen this person. He knows who it is."

"Fook," Niall said, summing things up nicely.

"There's a key," Eirik said, killing all doubt and bringing a round of harsh cursing to the room.

Tamil cringed. This wasn't good. He shouldn't have said anything, but they needed to know they weren't safe. He was so torn.

Jonathan leaned forward in his seat and focused on Eirik. "Do you know who it is?"

Eirik shook his head. "It would be a heavily guarded secret. One only Gods would know, you understand." A round of nodding scattered through the room, making Tamil wonder what they knew. They obviously shared a secret of their own. "If Tamil knows the way to the underworld and who holds the key, he'll never be safe. They'll never stop looking for him."

Jonathan stared Risk's way, but Tamil didn't think he saw anything other than whatever was inside his head. He shook his head. His wings expanded as he took a breath. "I think we have to assume he knows everything and start looking for ways to keep him safe."

Risk nodded. "I'll do whatever it takes. No way is Tamil returning to that place."

A sad look passed over Jonathan's features. "I think it's safe to say you probably won't ever see your home again. At least, not until we can deal with this or contain it."

Tamil's stomach dropped. From the moment he realized Risk was his blood mate, there'd never been any chance of Risk's life going back to normal. He should've been braver. Risk didn't deserve this. He'd been nothing but wonderful to Tamil. All Tamil had done was take. He should've already run, saved Risk from him.

Dougal cut in. "But this demon, that's nothing for you, Jonathan. You could rid the world of him with a snap of your fingers. We've seen it happen."

Jonathan made a helpless gesture. "I'd have to know where he is, and right now, I don't know where to start. If I let any of you out of my sight, and you get hurt, I'll never forgive myself."

Tamil backed away from the doorway and retraced his steps. Risk deserved to have his life back. The nice, quiet home he'd enjoyed before Tamil destroyed his peace. Jonathan deserved to be free of worrying over Pyro. Tamil was the one who'd brought him to their door. If he wasn't there, they could go back to their lives. Tamil would give it back to them. His eyes fell closed and his stomach churned. He could already feel the madness suffocating him. The burning flesh. His sanity slipping away. Tamil took a breath and shook it off. This time, he'd know it was no one's fault. This time, he had something that couldn't be stripped away. He ignored the voice that whispered there was nothing Pyro couldn't strip away.

Tamil dressed as quickly as possible. He didn't know how much time he had before Risk returned, but he knew he had to go before he lost his nerve. His hand hovered over the poppet. She was something they could take. He already knew it would break him when they ripped her from his hands. He would have to leave her behind. Tamil stroked her dress one final time. It was better this way. Better for everyone. He was nothing. They had a shot.

With nothing left to do except leave, Tamil cast a quick glance around the room he'd shared with Risk. It was the only time he could remember the pain being worthwhile. Soon, Hell would remedy that. Tamil almost made it to the edge of the property. A familiar scent tinged the wind. He froze. While turning in a slow circle, he searched the shadows. A large black wolf leapt from the trees. Tamil's heart jumped into his throat. The wolf transformed into a man before landing softly a foot away.

"Hey, Tam."

Tamil patted his chest, trying to slow his racing head as he stared at Evan's bright smile. "What are you doing out here? It's almost sunrise."

A line appeared between Evan's gorgeous eyes. "I'm a wolf. I like the sunrise. Bleidd is in with Jonathan and all the guys, so I decided to pounce on some grasshoppers. It's oddly satisfying when they crunch. Except I think I just accidentally squished a frog instead. Well..." Evan looked guilty. "I know I squished a frog. I had to find the hose."

"Oh." That was gross.

Evan's smile reappeared. "What are you doing out here? Did you get shooed from the room too?"

"I wasn't invited," Tamil admitted.

Evan looked genuinely insulted on his behalf. "That's mean. At least I got put out because I couldn't sit still. I get distracted easily," Evan admitted. "So, where are you headed? I'll go with you."

Panic had Tamil's heart racing. "You can't go with me. I think the meeting is almost over. You should go back to the house."

The way Evan eyed him had Tamil ready to bolt. Evan's gaze moved toward the house before settling on him again. "You're all alone and it looks like you're leaving the property. I don't think I should let you do that alone. It's not safe."

Tamil's shoulders fell. "Go back to your mate, Evan. You can't go where I'm going." Without further explanation, he walked away.

Evan fell into step beside him.

An aggravated-sounding huff escaped Tamil. "I'm serious, Evan."

Evan gave him a sharp nod. "Me too. It's not safe out there and if you won't be safe, I won't either."

Exasperation owned Tamil. "For the love of... I'm leaving, Evan. For good. You can't go with me."

"Why would you do that?" Evan asked, somewhere between a yell and a cry. "Risk loves you. He's your blood mate. Have you ever seen someone without their blood mate, especially one they love even without the blood bond? It's brutal."

Tamil didn't slow. "Where I'm going, it'll be like I'm dead."

"That's even worse," Evan cried, not letting up. "I was with Baptiste when Eirik died. It was horrible. You don't want to do that to Risk. It'll be like he died too."

"He's stronger than me." Even Tamil heard the desperation in his voice. "Risk can survive losing me. I can't survive losing him. If I stick around, he'll never get to go home. If he does, he could die, and my sanity isn't that strong. I couldn't survive it. I have to go so he can live." The panic had Tamil desperate. Before Evan could say anything else, Tamil changed into a bird.

Evan snatched him out of the air. "Ha. I knew all that butterfly chasing would come in handy." Evan smiled brightly while heading back toward the property line. "Everyone else is always like—stop staring out the window and chasing bugs, Evan. You need to be a man, but did you see me? I snatched you right out of the air. Ha."

Tamil turned back into a man, dropping to the ground and unbalancing Evan. Unfortunately, the move caused Evan to land on top of him, so he still couldn't get away.

"I don't want this, Evan. Go away."

Evan refused to budge. "You can just die mad about it." He looked panicked, as if realizing what he'd said. "Just don't die, okay?"

Tamil gave up trying to push Evan's heavy weight off him. He went limp. "Why are you doing this? I'm trying to save Risk."

"Because I'm your friend," Evan said, looking serious. "When things go down, friends do one of three things. A, they go with you. B, you go to jail together, or C, they stop you from being stupid. You're being stupid."

"Thanks for no—"

"I see you brought me a treat."

The blood froze in Tamil's veins. His gaze shot around, searching everywhere. Pyro stepped from the shadows. He was smooth perfection—like shiny glass meets old money. He wore an expensive suit. His hair was slicked back from his face. Pyro looked exactly like a man who'd bargain for a soul. Nothing about Pyro screamed monster, except his eyes, which glowed like flames, and his feral smile. But Tamil knew the real face behind the man; it was too horrible to look upon.

Tamil choked. "Run, Evan."

Evan didn't budge. He stared at Pyro, looking every bit as stunned and terrified as he should.

"Run, Evan," Tamil screamed, breaking the trance.

He felt Evan tense as if preparing to sprint. Instead, he turned wolf and sat on Tamil.

"You're a goddamn idiot," Tamil said, trying to breathe under the weight.

Pyro sprang. He snatched Evan up by the scruff as if he was no more than a puppy. "He smells like magic." Pyro leaned in and inhaled. His eyes fell closed. His perverse expression turned Tamil's stomach. "And untainted. Oh, Tamil," Pyro said, opening his eyes and focusing on Tamil. "You always have known just how to please me."

To Evan's credit, he didn't make a sound. Tamil feared what would happen if Evan drew too much attention to himself. Right now, Pyro's intent was to hurt Tamil. Evan was just a tool to that end. But he wouldn't hesitate to break Evan's neck if he struggled. Tamil pushed to his feet, trying to hide the way his whole body shook. He thought he'd known. He'd thought he'd been prepared to go back. There was no way to be ready for the pain or fear.

"Let him go, and I'll go with you without a fight."

The low, evil laugh that Pyro released at his claim made Tamil shake harder. "You won't fight either way." Pyro's flickering gaze swept Tamil's body. "You'll crawl to me and beg to go back, because you're already my bitch. There's no need to put on an act for the pup. He'll crawl too soon."

Bile rose in Tamil's throat. This was his fault. "Let him go," he repeated. He couldn't back down. Evan didn't understand. He was good. The things Pyro would do. Tamil couldn't take it. He couldn't know it was because of him. Evan was innocent.

"Oh, my sweet whore, you know I cannot." He stroked Evan's fur with his free hand. The lust in his expression crushed Tamil's throat. "He's so pretty. Imagine how he'll cry. That sweet puppy whine. Fuck, you know I can't resist."

Tamil's stomach heaved. "Let him go." Even Tamil heard the difference in his voice. His skin itched and stretched. He could feel his body changing. It was out of his control. Pyro looked his way and froze. Tamil took a step in his direction. Each one he took, he grew taller. In his rage, he didn't know himself. "Put the wolf down," Tamil growled, sounding inhuman even to his ears.

"You did it," Pyro said, sounding proud. "You got him to touch you. I knew you could do it."

He understood then. Tamil could only become some-thing or someone he'd touched. In his anger, he'd become Jonathan. That had been Pyro's plan all along. Set him free in the path of the most powerful being in existence. Then, Pyro would control someone equally powerful. He could do anything, even overthrow Hell. There was only one problem. Tamil controlled the power. Not him. And Pyro no longer controlled Tamil.

"I think I'm tired of this."

Pyro blinked, as if it hit him. He wasn't the strongest here. Not anymore. His grip loosened. Evan hit the ground and scrambled away. Tamil wasn't satisfied. Pyro would never leave. For the rest of their lives, Risk and Tamil would look over their shoulders, waiting for his next attack. It had to stop.

"You should've stayed in Hell."

"What—"

Tamil didn't let him finish. He snapped his fingers, unsure of what would happen. All he knew was that something would. Pyro exploded. Chunks of flesh flew in every direction. Acidic blood sizzled as it hit his skin before instantly healing.

He glanced around at the mess. Evan crawled out from underneath the brush where he'd hidden the moment Pyro dropped him. He looked shell-shocked but unharmed.

"I think we need to find that hose again," Tamil said for lack of anything else.

Evan nodded. "Yeah. Also, maybe we shouldn't tell anyone about this."

Tamil nodded. "Yeah." As one, they headed back toward the house.

"Bleidd will definitely not let me come back if he finds out."

Tamil nodded, starting to feel really gross. "Yeah. I imagine not."

Evan glanced his way. "You saved me."

Tamil cast a glance Evan's way. It felt shy, even to him. "I wouldn't let anything happen to you. Like you said, we're friends."

"Do you think I'll get the demon sickness? Since he touched me?"

Tamil shook his head. "You'd know. I think your thick fur saved you. You should probably rinse off too, just in case."

Thankfully, Evan knew exactly where the hose was. He poured water down Tamil's body. "It's really strange seeing you in Jonathan's body. It's like you're really him, but you're not, you know?" he said as he helped wash the gunk from Tamil's hair and ensured there was no blood on him.

Once he was clean, Tamil turned back into himself. He hadn't wanted to transform until the blood was gone in case it burned him. "I'd rather Jonathan never knew that. He already thinks I'm too powerful, and honestly, I don't want to do that again."

"I say we take this to the grave," Evan said, sounding serious.

Tamil nodded at the idea. "Yes. Definitely."

They shared a quick hug. It had Tamil turning shy again. He snatched up what was left of his clothes and hid them in the trash.

"I'd better get back in bed before I'm missed."

Evan nodded. "That's a good idea. Don't run away again, okay?"

Tamil nodded.

Evan gave him a sharp nod in return. "I need to sneak in too. You go through the back. I'll go in the front." With an agreement in place, they headed in different directions.

The moment Tamil was inside, he switched to stealth mode. Not only did he not want to get caught, he also didn't want to get caught in the nude. It hadn't seemed like a big deal with Evan. Evan was a wolf. Animals didn't care about clothes. Tamil, on the other hand, would have a hard time explaining why he wasn't wearing any.

When Tamil found the bedroom still empty, he breathed a sigh of relief. Instead of heading for the bed, he went straight for the shower. The hose had helped, but Tamil felt like Pyro's germs crawled on his skin. He had to get them off. As the hot water streamed down his skin, Tamil stared at nothing. Too many thoughts raced through his head to hang on to a single one. It was over. Pyro was the only person who knew his secret.

A chill raced through him. Tamil's body shook. He turned the water even hotter until it scalded his skin. Never again would anyone hurt him. Never again would he be forced into helplessness. He wished the knowledge would set him free. Instead, he felt nothing. There was no relief beyond no one else getting hurt. It felt like nothing at all.

Risk opened the shower door, startling him. His gaze shot to Risk's worried face. Guilt ate him alive on the inside. "Are you okay?"

Tamil nodded.

Risk chewed his bottom lip. His gaze moved over Tamil's face, as if looking for any sign he wasn't telling the truth. "Your skin is red—like you're scalding yourself."

"Sorry," Tamil said, rushing to turn down the heat. "I didn't realize."

"Is this because of me?"

Tamil's gaze shot to Risk's face. "What?"

Risk made a helpless gesture. "This. Are you..." He chewed his lip again before starting over. "Are you trying to wash me away?"

A wave of relief crashed over Tamil. This wasn't about what he'd done. "No. Not at all. I love you. I'd never want to wash you away." Horror overcame Tamil as he realized what he'd said.

Risk's smile was everything. "You love me?"

Tamil nodded. Fear owned him. If Risk wanted, he could break Tamil now in a way he'd never been broken. "I woke up alone." Tamil's voice shook.

A frown furrowed Risk's brow. "Jonathan called a meeting. Can I join you?" He hadn't lied about where he'd gone. Tamil felt like a terrible person.

"I'd like that."

Risk quickly stripped and stepped inside the shower. The moment their bodies met, Tamil's cock stirred. He couldn't get enough of the way Risk felt against him. It had nothing to do with Risk being his mate. He knew, even if they didn't have that bond, he'd want this man. Risk's mouth covered his. It was an explosion of heat. The cold shower wall touched Tamil's back. Risk massaged his ass, dragging the lower half of Tamil's body against his until their erections bumped. Their tongues stroked and twisted together, struggling to be as close as possible.

Risk leaned away, gasping for air. "I want to make love to you. I know you're not ready, but I need you to know you're wanted."

Tamil was on fire. The wisps of adrenaline from his run-in with Pyro still pumped through his veins. His fingers dug into Risk's arms. "I want you to make love to me. Please?"

"Are you sure?" Risk looked hopeful and turned on.

Tamil fought a growl. "Yes. Now."

Risk nodded. "Hold on." He disappeared and reappeared every bit as fast.

A chuckle escaped Tamil. "Where did you go?" Risk's skin was chilled, as if he'd been outside.

"To get this," Risk said, popping open a tube of lube with his teeth.

Tamil's stomach muscles clenched. The moment didn't feel real. He wasn't afraid. Risk belonged to him. He would keep Risk sated. Before Tamil could ask any more questions, Risk reclaimed his mouth.

His chilled skin was the only thing that had cooled. Tamil's cock leaked, begging for attention. In a show of Vampiric strength, Risk lifted Tamil with one arm. With his free hand, Risk toyed with Tamil's asshole, coating him with lube. Quick gasps escaped Tamil as he writhed against Risk's fingers. He'd never expected to like it. Everything else Risk did was amazing, and Tamil knew he'd enjoy pleasing Risk, but he'd never expected Risk's fingers to feel the way they did.

Every sensation was new. He'd never gotten to do this because he wanted to. It was like Risk was tickling him, but more. He wanted to move away, yet he didn't. Tamil closed his eyes and focused on Risk's touch. Risk kissed his neck, but Tamil could tell they were distracted kisses. Like Tamil, he was focused on the lower half of their bodies. Risk's fingers were replaced with something larger. His wide crown probed at Tamil's hole. Tamil was too fascinated to tense. He wanted it. His body gave, welcoming Risk. A moan escaped him as his dick jumped. Risk's cock stretched him and bumped something internal that had another moan falling from his lips.

"You're so hot," Risk whispered against his neck. "So hot and tight on my dick. Damn, Tamil. We just fit."

He understood. They did. Everything meant something now that they were together. He clung to Risk's large shoulders, letting Risk set the pace. With his back against the wall and Risk pumping inside him, Tamil couldn't think of anything else. The sensations happening to his body were everything. Over and over, Risk's dick massaged a spot inside him that had Tamil holding his breath. It was like his cock was getting rubbed and Tamil relished the building madness. Pressure beat at his crown. Risk's tongue swiped at his neck. Tamil wanted more. He wanted everything. Whimpers kept leaving him. He scratched at Risk's skin, winding tighter by the second. Tamil needed something, but he didn't know what. Just more. Risk's fangs brushed his throat. The moan that tore from Tamil's chest came from his soul. Risk did it again.

"Yes," Tamil breathed, wanting it. Needing Risk to pierce his skin. Connect them in every way. Crawl inside him.

Risk's fangs sank into his throat. He sucked. Tamil exploded. Stars popped behind his closed lids. Sounds he'd never made before poured from his mouth. Risk pumped deeper, giving Tamil his cum as he took his blood. They were one soul in that moment. Tamil knew peace like he never had. He died a little in Risk's arms.

Tamil's heart slowed as Risk let his feet slip to the floor. Their mouths sought and found each other. "I love you," Risk whispered against his lips, stealing the final piece of Tamil's heart. This man was Tamil's heaven. He knew. Tamil had already seen Hell. If anyone could tell the difference, it was him. Risk was everything good and perfect. Tamil was humbled in his arms.

Risk cleaned their bodies before wrapping Tamil in a fluffy towel and carrying him to bed. Under the blankets, their nude and overheated bodies molded together, fitting just as they should. Risk's chest felt perfect against Tamil's back. He snuggled closer, wiggling his ass against Risk's crotch, ensuring he got as close as possible. A contented sigh left his lips as his eyes fell closed. Now they could sleep. No more fear. Only new and happy memories to make.

CHAPTER
NINE

SOMEONE KNOCKING ON THE DOOR WOKE RISK. He didn't want to release Tamil to answer. The bed felt amazing—like they were wrapped in a heaven burrito. The knocking wouldn't stop. With a sigh, he rolled from the bed. He found a pair of shorts and pulled them on before answering. He tried opening the door as quietly as possible, hoping he didn't wake Tamil. Jonathan stood on the other side with Lire.

"Yeah?" Risk rubbed his eyes, trying to wake up.

"We found Pyro."

At Jonathan's announcement, Risk was awake. "What? You did?" The sun was still up. "Do you ever sleep?"

Lire snorted at the question. "We didn't have to search hard. I found him in chunks at the edge of the property just outside the warding."

Risk blinked several times. "That's... odd."

Lire nodded. "I caught wind of him while on patrol. Evan's and Tamil's scents were everywhere as well. Evan's, I get. He was outside during our meeting, running the property line. But Tamil, there's no reason for his scent to be out that far."

Risk turned. Tamil was sitting in the middle of the bed, watching them in silence. He looked sweet and sleep swollen. Risk wanted to rush to his side. Instead, he stood still and waited. Tamil's hand snaked beneath the blanket and came out with the poppet. His gaze never wavered from Risk. Risk hated that the man obviously felt the need for protection under their stares. Tamil toyed with the doll, running her dress through his fingers. He looked guilty.

"Jonathan said you could never go home."

Risk's shoulders fell. He'd overheard their meeting. "We didn't want you to worry."

"I know, but it's my job to worry about you. You love your home. I know what it cost you, and I can't be the reason you never get to go back there."

Risk shook his head. He didn't understand why Tamil didn't realize he didn't care if he ever saw that place again as long as he had Tamil. He had a horrible feeling Tamil had risked breaking Risk's heart to ensure he could go home. "Sweetie, I don't give a damn about anything as much as your safety. Being with you, it's everything to me. If I have to stay here forever to have you, that's what I'll do."

Jonathan cut in. "I just really want to know why there're demon chunks killing our grass."

Tamil visibly swallowed. "You said Risk couldn't go home."

"Note to self," Lire said, sounding dry. "Don't tell Risk he can't go home."

Risk took a breath. He rubbed the spot between his eyes, trying to wrap his brain around the magnitude of what he'd obviously missed. He dropped his hand and focused on Tamil. "Are you okay, at least?"

Tamil nodded. "Am I in trouble?"

"No, baby."

"No, not at all," Jonathan and Lire said at the same time behind him. Everyone moved to the bed, obviously feeling the same desperation to comfort Tamil as Risk did.

Risk climbed in and wrapped his arms around Tamil. "Just maybe don't take on a demon prince without telling anyone again. Obviously, you are capable, but damn, baby, it scares me to think what could've happened. It would kill me if you got hurt. I love you. Please don't get hurt."

Jonathan rubbed Tamil's thigh while Lire rubbed Jonathan's back, as if comforting Tamil by proxy. "We were just scared for you when we realized what happened," Jonathan said, reassuring him. "Also, I really think we need to get those lessons started with Baptiste. If you learn how to control these powers, imagine how your life could be. You'll never have to be afraid again."

Tamil shook his head. "I have Risk for that. Of course, I'll still work with Baptiste, but I have Risk. I'm not scared anymore. The idea of Pyro touching him." Tamil shook his head. "I couldn't take it. I don't know what happened."

Risk held on. This man was more powerful than Risk could wrap his head around. He scared Risk, but not for the reasons he probably should. Just as Jonathan had warned, Tamil didn't love himself. He had no self-preservation. Risk needed everyone to leave. The panic eating his stomach rose by the second. He needed to check Tamil for injuries, ensure he was okay in every way. It didn't matter to his over-reacting brain that they'd been sleeping peacefully for hours since Tamil had apparently blown up a demon. Risk needed to be alone with Tamil.

Obviously sensing his panic, Jonathan stood. "We'll let you go back to sleep. We just wanted to make sure you were okay. Thank you for saving me a headache. I think I'll sleep in tomorrow," Jonathan said, heading for the door. "Dang," he added, sounding bright. "Imagine how much easier my life will be when you're helping me. I might get to go on a date with my mates. Oh, the possibilities," Jonathan sang as he led Lire from the room.

The moment the door closed behind them, Risk urged Tamil onto his back. He wrapped the man in his arms and held him tight against his chest. Risk buried his face in the crook of Tamil's neck and inhaled. The scent of his mate soothed his racing heart. "I love you so much," Risk breathed against his skin.

Tamil rubbed Risk every place he could reach. "I'll never let anyone hurt you."

A surprised laugh escaped Risk. "You're amazing." He placed several loud kisses to Tamil's neck, trying to placate his needy heart. "Promise me you'll keep yourself safe. For me, please. I don't think you understand how much I need you."

Tamil turned his head and kissed Risk's nose. "I promise."

Risk stared into the blue eyes like a summer's day that had completely stolen him. He had no choice but to trust Tamil that he'd try to stay in one piece. He could say one thing for certain, life with Tamil would be anything but boring. At least, he'd never been happier, but they were definitely not getting out of bed for a while. Risk's old heart couldn't take another shock for a while.

KEEP an eye out for the next book in the series, Yearn.

Please consider leaving a review at the retailer where this book was purchased. Reviews really help with a book's visibility, which ensures I can continue writing. Thank you, Charity.

ABOUT THE AUTHOR

Charity Parkerson is an award winning and multi-published author with several companies. Born with no filter from her brain to her mouth, she decided to take this odd quirk and insert it in her characters.

*Seven-time Readers' Favorite Award Winner

*2015 Passionate Plume Award Finalist

*2013 Reviewers' Choice Award Winner

*2012 ARRA Finalist for Favorite Paranormal Romance

*Five-time winner of The Mistress of the Darkpath

Connect with her online:

--Join my street team: facebook.com/TeamCharityParkerson

--Sign up for my newsletter: http://bit.ly/CharityNews

--Website: charityparkerson.com

--Facebook: facebook.com/authorCharityParkerson

facebook.com/TheMenofSin

--Twitter: twitter.com/CharityParkerso